Memories and Sometimes Sorrow

Victor M. Sandoval

Sandoval, Victor M.

Memories and Sometimes Sorrow

Cover design and illustration by Victor M. Sandoval

Summary: In *Rock Salt and Time*, a young man returning from war deals with the end of his marriage and the death of a combat friend.

My Little Sister finds siblings resolving the growing distance between them after the death their father.

In *Hail, the Champ* ,a twelve-year-old girl, a loving daughter in a fragile family, is the winning contestant on the "Hail, the Champ" television show.

ISBN: 9780578740997

Contents

"All happy families are alike; each unhappy family is unhappy in its own way."

_____ Leo Tolstoy

∿∿ ∿∿

Rock Salt and Time

Mundo came home from the war in November. All the leaves had fallen from the apricot tree near the front porch where he sat thinking and forgetting, mostly forgetting. Forgetting about Lucha.

Lucha was the dark-haired girl that lived next door. With her long slender arms and legs, she caught Mundo's eye, like a kite tangled in the branches of a tree. She got along with the girls, but she got along with the boys better. Her father didn't approve. He was strict with her, often pulling her by the hair from the front yard, back inside where he knew she would be safe. At seventeen, she married Mundo to get out of the house. Everyone knew that, everyone, except Mundo.

Three weeks after they were married, Mundo was inducted into the army. He shipped out to Korea and then wrote to her all the time and sent pictures too. But one day, Mundo received a letter from Lucha. She wrote that she was very sorry, but she had found someone else and would not be there when he got home.

Sitting next to Mundo was his grandfather. Grandpa relaxed in an old chair that he brought from Mexico made of pine boughs stripped bare and bent, held together with nails and glue. He sat on a soft feather pillow and a corduroy cushion at his back. A small table at his side had his favorite red clay jarro of ice water.

Mundo stared at the fifty-year-old barren apricot tree, more than twice as old as he. Its massive trunk came straight out of the ground like a forearm exploding through the earth with a handful of branches clawing the sky.

"Did it give fruit?" Mundo asked as if spoken words only got in the way of their being together.

"No, not this year. Nada, nothing but pink blossoms, bonitas, that danced on the wind, all around, leaving these little furry green pods the size of piñones that shriveled up and fell to the ground." He measured off the tip of his wrinkled pinky finger with his yellow thumbnail.

"Maybe it's dead. It's done. Too old to give fruit anymore." Mundo rubbed his forehead as if grinding an evil thought away.

"Lo creo," Grandpa spoke, brushing back the hairs of his mustache dampened by drops of water.

"Tomorrow, I'll cut it down and dig it out by the roots." Mundo moved forward in his chair, letting his black hair fall over the left side of his face.

"It's a lot of work." Grandpa stared at the aged tree, the one he planted as a seedling for his wife's sake. She wanted fruit. He wanted shade.

"I need to do something." Mundo looked into his hands, growing soft with disuse.

"Lo creo, que si." Grandpa tasted the air with a long sigh.

"Tomorrow then. I'll start early and not stop till I'm done. Gotten rid of that old thing." Mundo shook his head from side to side. "Do you remember the swing you made for me out of rope and an old tire? Remember, Grandpa?"

"Como no." Grandpa's brown teeth emerged between his thin lips and made a weathered smile.

"And what about those slick slingshots that you taught me how to make by cutting just the right branches where they made a "v" so I could tie the rubber bands to the leather sling made from an old shoe tongue. Remember?" Mundo stood up and gripped the porch rail.

"Si." Grandpa nodded and nothing more.

"And that spring when it grew so much fruit that the branches snapped from the weight of it. There was a great cracking sound, like a shotgun, that scared everyone out of their houses looking for the shooter."

"De veras." Grandpa reached for the old clay jarro, poured a cup, and gulped down a full swallow.

"And I still can feel the swat in the pants you gave me for carving letters into the trunk on a Saturday night after getting my first kiss. 'Mundo loves Lucha' inside a heart with an arrow through it. I'll bet it's still there." Mundo's voice trailed off as he stepped forward and stretched his neck to see from this distance. Then he stepped down from the porch and walked to the tree.

He searched with his eyes and fingertips along the chocolate brown trunk. He found that the tree's bark had healed over the words, leaving scars, hard scabs, ringed by soft, dried blisters of sap the color of honey.

The next day Grandpa sat on the porch and watched as Mundo carried the tools he would need over his muscular shoulders: the spade for digging, the ax for cutting. In his right hand, he clutched the bow saw. Mundo approached the old apricot tree like an enemy in his path. He set his tools down, except for the saw that now was part of him. He climbed an old wooden ladder that had been propped against the tree trunk many months ago by Grandpa, eager to climb but too old to do so without fear. Mundo mounted the ladder, braced himself near the top step, and began whipping the bow saw back and forth into the meat of the lowest branch. The sawdust gathered about the steel blade; the leading edge scalloped like a shark's grin.

Mundo stepped higher up the ladder as he made his way to the next limb. The morning air was chilly, but his body heat forced sweat from his brown skin in regular, even waves that became sprinkled by moist pulp and fine timber dust. Hour by hour, the sun rose high in the sky as Mundo climbed toward it, losing himself in the net of branches until he cut off all the foe's branches. Finished, he stood tall on the ladder and looped his bow saw around a fresh stub, letting it swing to and fro like a storefront shingle announcing, "Mundo, Topper of Trees."

"Cuidado, mi'jo, don't fall." Grandpa lifted the red jarro toward him in a gesture of shared triumph.

The denuded apricot tree was now a tight gnarled fist attached to a stiff, coarse wooden arm thrust into the sky from the earth below. Mundo stepped down from the ladder and put the saw away, gathered the fallen branches into bundles that he tied with a hemp rope. He then confronted the aged trunk, a singular poised muscle, useless, and no longer a tree, maybe a fence post, but not a tree. He kicked at it with his leather army boot, hoping beyond hope that it would give, lean a bit, and signal defeat. It didn't. After all, it was rooted to the spot, and how foolish to think otherwise.

But Mundo had planned well. He began digging at the trunk base, cutting through the small surface roots with the spade's sharp, pointed end. Now the bold roots started to surface as the shovel's face, under the weight and power of Mundo's thick boot sole, slid deep into the surrounding earth. The stubborn knotty roots, unmolested, showed themselves but gave away nothing. Mundo stopped digging. He placed his hands, one atop the other, at the end of the shovel handle, then rested his chin on his hands and studied what he'd done. Like a dry moat around the foot of the tree, the excavation uncovered an array of wooden spokes radiating from the trunk like spidery legs.

Mundo took in a deep breath as an image rose before him of Private Rojas floating, face down, in a pool of shallow water. Sunlight sparkled from his watchband, visible below the deep green rippling shadows cast in the late Korean afternoon.

Mundo stabbed the shovel into the ground and severed smaller roots that, relieved of their tension, coiled back. They revealed a massive anchoring growth, a root the thickness of a man's thigh that plunged into the ground, disappearing into the depths.

Mundo remembered meeting Frank Rojas in boot camp, stateside. Rojas was always in trouble. Breaking the rules and getting caught, but he had an excuse. He explained it like this, "Hey, I'm 'Rojas.' You know the 'red' one. I stand out. Look, Moreno or Val Verde, Private Brown, and Private Green cut up too, but never get caught. No one ever sees them. No one notices them. Just me, bright red Rojas." He would roll his "r's" and shadow box for a minute or two, then finish by putting the fingertips of both his hands to his chest and quickly pulling them away, as if touching a hot iron placa. The two of them became friends in no time. Mundo talked a lot about his wife Lucha back home. Rojas listened and joked, "Does she have a sister?"

Mundo drove the spade into the ground with his foot, trying to expose the wooden muscle. He dug around it and beneath it until he stood deep in a hole with only the great arm of the root naked, bare, like a neck readied for the blade of a bayonet.

By chance, Mundo and Rojas were assigned to the same unit and shipped out to Camp Charlie in Tongduchon, South Korea. All the other recruits knew Rojas's reputation for causing trouble. When Rojas screwed up, they all suffered for it. In the army, "it's all for one, and one for all." That's just the way it was, running an extra five miles, assigned extended K.P., restricted to base with no leaves. Everyone suffered for Rojas. But they accepted it. Rojas was a funny, likable guy. Besides, a "better him than me" grin embraced everyone's face whenever Rojas got caught.

Mundo trusted Rojas with his thoughts about Lucha: how much he missed his beautiful wife and how they grew up together, were neighbors, went to school together, and were friends before becoming lovers.

Mundo climbed out of the hole, walked over to the porch where the ax, the "asesino," the killer, stood leaning awkwardly against the porch steps. Mundo picked it up, felt its heft, brought the head of the ax to his face, and examined the sharpened edge, shiny and thin. He carried it over his shoulder to the stump and climbed into the hole with the root. He braced his legs in the hollow space, brought the ax above his head, aimed, and swung the deadly steel weight down into the flesh of the root that gave way to flying splinters of skin that revealed a deep cut.

Mundo laughed, not at himself for falsely thinking the root would give in, sever into two pieces with his first blow. Then he smiled at the remembrance of the camp guard tower on twenty-foot-high wooden stilts that exploded into bits and pieces, smithereens. Rojas, drunk with the local hooch, ran his half-track full speed into it because the guy on duty in the tower had fingered him the day before when he headed into town without permission. The C.O. restricted the entire platoon for a month because of it.

Mundo spent time writing to Lucha every day. He would tell her about his friend, "the troublemaker" Rojas, and his latest prank, hoping to make her laugh.

Mundo brought the ax above his head, grunted, and plunged the edge into the root again and again until he cut through. The root surrendered its hold to the earth, one end choosing the stump, the other the ground. Now, a space with an ax head's thickness kept the severed root ends apart once and for all.

Eventually, the restrictions were over, and all the guys in the outfit were free to leave camp, but for only a day. Rojas said he knew of a place deep in the jungle where cool water pooled beneath dangling vines and young virgins washed their clothes. Everyone laughed but went along with it. They jumped into their jeeps and half-tracks and drove for over an hour to get there. It didn't matter. They were on free time. After a month of restriction, the soldiers let the hooch flow without end as they drove the narrow winding roads at full throttle. When they arrived at the place, it was everything Rojas promised it would be. Lush growth surrounded pools of calm, shallow water. In no time, the G.I.s were stripped down to nothing, playing grab-ass, joking, laughing, and drinking like there was no tomorrow.

In the late afternoon, Mundo was the first to spot Rojas floating face down in the water.

"Knock it off, Rojas," Mundo called out and threw a leafy twig at him. The twig landed on his back, the leaves clinging to his wet skin.

"Rojas," Mundo shouted.

Several other soldiers bolted upright where they sat at the edge of the water. Mundo jumped to his feet, ran into the water, and struggled against the water's weight seizing his legs. Nearing Rojas, he reached out and pulled his body out of the water. Now other hands were there to help. They pounded his chest. They slapped his back. They blew air into his lungs, but nothing would revive him. Rojas was dead? This was no joke. This time. This time....

"Shit, shit, shit." Mundo moaned.

Now others came and saw Rojas cradled in Mundo's arms.

"What the hell? What happened?" A soldier asked.

"It's Rojas. He's not breathing. He's drowned. He's dead." Another answered.

"What are we going to do?"

"What are you talking about? Do?"

"Look, if we go back now, it's over. Do you know what I mean? There'll be an investigation. We'll be restricted again, for months, and we just got out, just got permission for leaves."

"What are you talking about?"

"Why can't we stay here a little longer? It won't make any difference. Why let Rojas ruin our good time again. We won't have another chance for a long time. Damn it, a long time."

"Rojas." Mundo cupped his face in his hands and sobbed.

Hour after hour, Mundo swung the heavy ax over and over again, slicing roots all around the base of the stump. He used the spade to dig deeper and deeper. He exposed the hidden roots to the light of day; then killed them. The tree stump must go.

Mundo remembered that Rojas had only been dead a week when the mail came flying into his bunk, one letter, the last letter, from Lucha. No perfume, only tear stains on smeared ink--- his.

But the stump clung to the earth. When Mundo felt sure the stump was cut free and rootless, he swung the head of the asesino, with all his might, into the tree stump, but the rigid post did not give. Mundo's ears alone echoed with an intense thud, vibrating up from the ground, over and over again, a question without an answer.

It was dusk now. Grandpa walked over to Mundo and put his arm around him.

"Mi'jo, the taproot runs straight and deep into the ground where you can't reach it." Grandpa counseled.

"How then?" Mundo asked. "I gotta get it out."

"In the garage, there's a bag of rock salt. Bring it here and pour it into the hole around the roots of the tree. Flood it with water, and in time the roots will shrivel up, and the stump will fall free on its own." Grandpa knew what to do.

Mundo did as he was told.

When he had finished, he joined Grandpa on the porch, sat next to him, and stared out at what was left of that stubborn apricot tree, waiting, forgetting.

My Little Sister

Maya, Victor's younger sister, was mad at him, but he wasn't sure why.

"When are you coming up to visit me? You like Santa Rosa. I know you do. When are you coming?" Her voice surged through the phone line, a measured crescendo that would not be denied.

"Soon," Victor said as he sat stone still at his writing desk, looking down at the stack of student papers that needed correcting. He was about to make some excuse why he couldn't visit her, but he thought about the three-day holiday weekend coming up. Arroyo High School, where he taught, would be closed on Monday.

And now, thinking about it, he knew she had every right to be mad at him. It had been seven years since he had visited her in Santa Rosa. She hadn't forgotten. She knew Victor had no real reason for not accepting and not acting on her many invitations over the years. Victor had always responded with "maybe's" or "I'll try's," but she knew that those were his feeble attempts at saying "No." But this time, Victor sensed a life and death urgency in her voice.

"Well, are you coming up?"

"Yes," Victor responded, wondering whose life was going to be saved.

Leaving the San Francisco Airport, Maya drove home on a chilly August night while Victor recited poems from a book she had given him a month ago for his birthday.

Looking out at the night sky, Victor felt the darkness captured them, and the silence linked them like it used to be when they were younger. He knew what she was thinking, and she knew his thoughts. He was five years older than she was, but she always acted as if she were, well, his age.

He remembered an adult education class in photography that they took together. She was only sixteen but loved learning new things. When she discovered how to take a "double exposure," she filled her photo albums with ghostly images of headshots floating above trees, garden flowers, and grassy hillsides. She especially loved the double exposure of their father, smiling, through the branches of a leafy avocado tree that grew in front of their house.

It was their father's death that tore the family apart. Although Victor tried his best to keep everyone together, he knew Maya blamed him.

When they reached her house, a converted wooden farm shed, she clicked on the light of a chrome studio lamp arched over a gray couch. Windows draped with globes of the earth and constellations surrounded the tiny room. On shelves stood a pink ceramic hand with red fingernails, a kaleidoscope, and a stack of unused French-fry cartons. On a small table near the door sat a small basket filled with flower petals. This alone confirmed Victor's suspicions of the Bohemian lifestyle that he thought she lived.

"Coffee or tea?" She nodded her forehead at Victor, bringing a strand of dark satin hair across her tan cheek.

She ground the coffee in a small electric grinder for herself. Then, she scooped a bit of peppermint and chamomile tea from a used fruit jar into a ceramic tea-ball with a tiny silver chain for Victor.

"Do you want the bedroom or sleep out here on the couch?"

Victor settled for the couch, feeling gallant and needing more time to get used to the surroundings. Alone in the dark, Victor could see an empty birdcage, an oil painting on her bedroom door, the bentwood rocker, a pair of skates, a gas heater, antique oak mirrors, seashells, a stereo, and several Hallmark cards. One was a "Thank You" note that Victor had sent.

Funny how different we've grown, Victor thought. The last time he saw her, she was a first-year college girl, waitressing, rooming with a girlfriend, living a carefree life far away from home. And Victor, on the other hand, was recently graduated and looking for a teaching job. But now, things were quite different.

The next morning after breakfast, Victor watched Maya as her body's thin line coiled about the chair and table as she worked on a calculator. Then she telephoned her employee and scheduled the week's work on a notepad. Later Maya explained that her partner, Carol, was vacationing in Mexico. That meant she would have her hands full all morning running the business, Sonoma Salsa, by herself.

For the next several hours, Victor went with her while she dickered with the local produce supplier and asked the bank to deposit surplus profits in a CD after weighing an interest-bearing account's merits versus the business checking liquidity account. Lastly, at a leased grammar school kitchen, she set to work, delegating cutting of onions and parsley to him and washing utensils to Brenda's lone employee. Next, like a medieval Merlin, Maya hovered over vats of chili salsa, mixing and stirring with a long-handled wooden spoon. Then she hand-poured the liquid gold into small containers ready for grocery store shelves.

That afternoon, she took Victor to her friend's apple orchard on a hill. As they climbed, their boots sank into the rain-swollen earth. They hiked up through the trees in silence. Near the top of the knoll, past the last row of trees, they turned to look at the pristine view. All around, verdant hills bordered an ocean-blue sky, marbled with swelling vanilla clouds, spewing from the jagged, green line of the horizon. Their eyes were full as they bit into the apples picked along the way.

More silence.

"Why did you abandon us?" Maya said.

"What are you talking about?" Victor said.

"Why did you leave the family?" Maya said. "When we needed you the most."

"You know why."

"No, tell me again."

"You really want to know why?" Victor stared into her eyes. "Do you?

"Victor, tell me."

"Mom asked me to leave."

"What?"

"She thought it was best that I leave so that she could start again with Daniel. After Dad died, she was lonely. It had been two years with both of us trying to hold the family all together. Then Daniel came along. He was a good man. He was good to you and Barbara. You know he was."

"I didn't . . . ," Maya hung her head.

"Besides, mom wanted me to have a chance to do whatI wanted to do. To get out there on my own, go back to school."

"What about me?" Maya said.

"You still had a year of high school left. You needed to graduate from high school. It was important."

"You know I wanted to go with you."

"That was impossible. You must be able to see that now."

"All I see now is that I wanted to run away after youleft us. I did the right thing, moving out as soon as I could. Moving, that's what I remember—getting the hell out."

"Maya, why are you so angry?"

"I'm mad at you, and I have every right to be."

"Really? Mad at me? I don't think so."

"Oh, sure. That's right, and you're Mr. Goody Two Shoes. I can't be mad at you, Mr. Wonderful, successful teacher."

"You're angry, alright, but not at me."

"Oh, I get it. You think I'm mad at myself for leaving my sisters, my family behind."

"No."

"Who then?"

"You're mad at Dad."

"Are you crazy? He's dead."

"Exactly. You're mad because he died. He left us."

Maya cast her eyes downward as if she didn't want to see what was in front of her. Her dark hair fell like a curtain, revealing nothing. Her body began to tremble, and she began to sob. Victor held her in his arms.

Victor was glad he came. His visit *had* been a matter of life and death.

Maya held Victor's hand as they walked down the soggy hill through the orchard.

Hail, the Champ

Irma, Robert, Rosie

Chapter One

The letter came late that afternoon. Rosie tore it open, jumped in the air, and ran outside.

"Hey, Mundo. Hey Baby Oscar. Look what I got in the mail," Rosie shouted, loud enough to get the attention of the boys playing football in a dirt lot. She waved the letter in the air like a banner.

Stopping the game, they gathered around her that late November afternoon.

"What you got?" asked Mundo, the oldest. He removed a cracked and chipped football helmet from his head.

"I won. I won. I'm going to be on 'Hail the Champ,' on television."

"Let's see," Mundo said, grabbing the letter from her. "You are. They did pick your name. You could win the bike. I sent in ten wrappers. How many did you send?"

"I sent in twenty-one," screamed Baby Oscar, eleven years old, sucking his thumb.

"So what, I didn't ask you," Mundo said. "Rosie?"

"One," Rosie said, "Only one."

"It figures. You're the luckiest person. You're always so lucky."

"I know. I know," Rosie replied, taking the letter back.

"Does Robert know you got picked?" Mundo asked.

"No."

"Just wait till your brother finds out," Mundo said, "He wants that bike bad."

Rosie cracked her knuckles. Then, she shifted her weight from one foot to another as a fistful of aggies, puries, and steelies bulged from her jeans' front pocket, and a soiled string from a spinning top and bubble gum baseball cards overflowed in the back.

"Let's play football." Mundo let the matter slip away as he ran his stubby fingers through his coarse hair.

In tribute to her good fortune, he offered his helmet to her. She put it on after she gathered her hair in a ponytail with a rubber band. On the first play, she carried the ball through the center of the line, bullying her way over would-be tacklers. She knew that what she lacked in strength, she gained in determination.

Hours later, at dusk, she saw her Dad, Manny, park his car near the wooden front door stoop. Watching him from the huddle, she saw him stand by the door, his gray trucker's uniform ringed with sweat, the L.A. Times under his arm, and a lunch pail in his hand. A handsome man in his thirties, Manny had smooth brown skin, which complemented the straight rows of white teeth that made his smile. She realized the dark moving forms of the football players had caught his attention and held him. She wanted to show him what she could do.

"Give me the ball." She took it around right end, avoided the grasps of two tacklers, and ran over a third, zig-zagging her way downfield to a touchdown. From the end zone, she saw Manny grin, shake his head, and enter the house.

She ran after him, opening the door just as he put his lunch pail down and asked his wife: "Who is that kid in the helmet outside playing football?"

"Dad, Dad, look at my letter," Rosie said, rushing into the living room with the helmet tilted back on her head.

"Was that you playing football out there? With those boys?" Manny said, turning to look at her. "What's wrong with you? Don't you know better than that?" He faced Rosie's Mother. "Look at your daughter. Don't you have any shame?" Manny clenched his fists to his sides.

"Rosie, go to your room," shouted her Mother, trying to save her. Lost, scared, Rosie did not move. "Rosie, go to your room now!" Rosie edged away.

****

Later she heard footsteps approach the curtained entrance to her bedroom. Robert used his forearm to sweep back the curtain as he walked in.

"What's wrong?" Robert asked, holding a neatly-rolled cotton apron beneath his arm. He waited for her sobbing to stop. "Rosie?"

"I. . .I. . .I. . ." Rosie cried, burying her head in the pillow that she held with both arms to her breasts.

"I should've known something was wrong when I first came into the house." Robert sat next to her on the lower bunk bed. "Dad's food was on the table getting cold while he sat reading the newspaper." She felt his strong arm about her shoulders. "Today at the store at work, when I was sweeping the floor near the soup can shelves, I found a quarter." Robert began to stroke Rosie's hair. "Right away, I told Mr. Ramos about it. Do you know what he said? He said to keep it. It's your reward, he said. 'A reward for what? Finding it? ' I asked. He said, 'For being honest.' How 'bout that?" Rosie nodded her head on the pillow. "Well, you know what I did with it? I bought five PowerHouse Candy Bars, and I'm going to give three of them to you." Robert pushed the candy bars into Rosie's hands. "Anyway, I have enough wrappers sent in already, and you only have one."

Rosie sat up, turned to Robert, hugged him, and cried even more than before.

"Wait, I thought that'd make you feel better," Robert said, patting her on the back. "Why are you crying?"

"I don't know. I wish I didn't have to cry. He always makes me cry so easy. Why? Nobody else can make me cry. Just him."

"Who? Dad?"

"Yeah . . . He got mad at me because I was playing football," Rosie sobbed as she reached in her back pocket for the letter.

"Oh, he thinks the guys will . . . he doesn't . . . it's okay." Robert wiped tears from her cheeks. "Don`t cry. I don't like to see you cry."

"Here, look at this." She handed the letter to him. She watched him slowly take the letter out and read it.

"You won. You won." Robert whispered. "I can't believe it." He clutched the bedpost with his free hand and squeezed until his knuckles turned white. His muscular arm poised, blue veins surfacing.

"It's true," Rosie said.

"Why didn't they pick me?" His course brown hair fell over his eyes as he turned his head.

"They still might."

"No, they won't." Robert shoved the candy bars aside.

"Oh, Robert, you go then."

"I can't. It was your wrapper."

"But you bought it for me, remember?"

"That doesn't make any difference. The bike . . ."Robert stopped himself, tugging at his shirt sleeve. "What did Dad say?"

"I don't think he knows yet."

"Wait, shhh, listen." Robert looked toward the curtain. "They're arguing. Let's see."

Following Robert, Rosie crouched down on the floor as he crawled to a hole near the bottom of the curtain that separated them from the living room where the shouting began. Rosie found a jagged tear in the cloth from which to watch.

"No, not my daughter," said Manny, sitting at the dinner table. He made the L.A. Times bark and snap as he folded the front page back and swept his knuckles across the fold, creating a thin crease.

Rosie saw her Mother, like a ghost, approach the table, moving silently on worn slippers. Her Mother's faded cotton-print dress was loose-fitting and had folds that swirled behind her when she moved. Beads of sweat rolled across her brow and dampened the nests of gray hairs at her temples as she placed the re-heated plate of rice and beans in front of him.

"Where's my fork?" said Manny, gathering in the plate. His wife returned with the fork. After placing it on the table, she hovered to the left and behind him.

"It's a boy's show. It's a show for boys. She should be ashamed of herself." Even before tasting the food, Manny demanded, "Salt. Where's the salt?"

After getting the salt shaker, her Mother resumed her silent vigil, her quiet appeal. Her small brown eyes and thin lips were still and calm, but the wrinkles that netted her face, Rosie felt, were alive with something strong, and one day she hoped to understand what that was.

"How would you get there? Hollywood?And the money for the streetcar?" He sprinkled a generous amount of salt over his food.

Her Mother only blinked. Rosie knew the end was near. Tears welled in the crooks of her Mother's eyes.

"All right, all right. Don't cry. I can't stand to see you cry. You take her. You take her," Manny shouted, shoveling a forkful of rice into his mouth. "<u>Mira</u>! Look now. The food's salty. Did you salt it before? Why didn't you tell me? You know I can'teat salty food."

Newspaper in hand, he rose from the table and retreated to his comfortable chair.

Rosie felt Robert's eyes on her. She turned to face him.

"Well, I guess I'll help you practice the different races and games played on 'Hail the Champ,'" Robert said, returning to the bed.

"You will?"

"Sure. After all, if you're going to be on the show, you have to do good and win."

"Oh, Robert, I always wanted a bike of my own, like yours, to go riding with you and the rest of the gang."

"Well, it looks like you'll have your chance."

"Do you think," Rosie asked, sitting beside him now, "I could try riding down Hazard Hill?"

"What? Hazard Hill? Are you crazy?" Robert's face softened. " We'll see. You're a good bike rider, but besides, you have to win the bike first." He grinned.

****

Later that night, in her bedroom, Rosie filled her March of Dimes card with the coins Robert had saved for her. She thought about her sister Irma in the County General Hospital's polio ward. Rosie tucked the card under her pillow, got in bed, and closed her eyes; then, as if in a dream, Rosie heard hushed voices arguing in another room. Her Mother's voice was like a birdcall, high and firm, and her Dad's was like a drum roll, angry and stern. Rosie could only catch a word or syllable every now and again. Still, the voices' broken rhythm let her know that it was a tug-of-war with words about her-- about going, or not going, on the television show. Soon the muted tones stopped, and Rosie fell asleep.

The next morning, Mother motioned with her hand for Rosie to come to her just before Rosie walked out of the house to school.

"Rosie, you need to wear something nice for the show." Mother said.

"What? What do you mean?" Rosie replied.

"You need to wear a dress." Mother combed back loose strands of hair behind her ear.

"A dress," Rosie said. "Why can't I wear what I always wear?"

"Because, because you're going to be on television." Mother said. "And lots of people will be watching you. And you want to look nice."

"But on the show, I have to run and jump against the boys. I can't wear a dress and do that." Rosie said. "Besides, I don't have a nice dress, really."

"I know, I know, but your Dad says you have to wear a dress or you can't go on TV," Mother said.

"Can't go?" Rosie asked. "Can't go?" The words "Can't go" exploded in her brain, like a backyard piñata cracked open, letting her dreams, brightly wrapped candies, drop to the ground and scatter in all directions, never, never to return.

"Don't worry." Her Mother went on. "I asked your Grandma if you could borrow one from your Aunt Bertha. She has lots of dresses. It will be okay."

"Oh, mama. Do I have to?" Rosie pleaded. But Rosie saw in her Mother's hazel eyes the answer simply and plainly.

Chapter Two

Rosie opened the rear door of the Chevy as soon as the tires rested at the curb. She saw Grandma Cuca standing on the wide porch with her arms crossed, unsmiling. Her strong figure, clothed in a sleeveless dress, stood rooted like an aged saguaro cactus. She wore her black hair with snake trails of gray pulled back from her face.

Rosie climbed out of the rear seat and closed the heavy door. Then she arched her body to look into the car and wave goodbye to her Mother. She tried to catch her Dad's eyes, but he held on to the steering wheel and stared straight ahead. Rosie didn't know why Grandma Cuca didn't like her Dad. No one ever talked about it. All she knew was that Grandma Cuca called him "Severo," the strict one, and he didn't like it. But Grandma somehow held her Mother to blame. After all, she married him.

When Rosie turned and stepped along the walkway that led to the house, the car sped off. She felt anxious about being here alone. Still, she knew that her parents would return in a few hours after buying the week's groceries at Grand Central Market downtown.

When Rosie reached the top step of the large wooden porch, she felt Grandma Cuca's firm hand at her back, pushing her into the house. Inside, the living room was cold and dark. She looked at the thick drapes that shut out all light, hanging from black iron rods with round ends shaped like bird claws.

"Here, mi'ja, say something to your Abuelita." Grandma Cuca led her by the hand to a rocking chair where Grandma Cuca's ninety-year-old mother sat like a dark shadow. Abuelita raised her gnarled, bony hand from her lap. She held in her other hand a black-beaded rosary that wound around her fingers like a serpent as she counted out her penance with a yellow thumbnail.

"Abuelita, this is Quetta's daughter, Rosie." Grandma Cuca said. Rosie reached out for Abuelita's hand and bent down to kiss her cheek. Rosie heard her whisper something in Spanish that she didn't understand, but Grandma Cuca nodded in agreement. Rosie remembered that after one of her few visits, she had asked why Abuelita always wore black. Her Mother explained that Abuelita was a superstitious woman who believed she had to dress for death because "Cuando llegue la muerte, quiero estar lista. When Death comes, I want to be ready to go."

"How is Irma doing?" Grandma Cuca asked. "Is she coming home soon from the hospital, pobrecita?"

"Soon, she's coming home soon," Rosie answered with a smile.

"You must miss your big sister a lot." Grandma Cuca said. "Mira, let's see if your Aunt Bertha is off the phone. She hasn't been out of her room all morning." Grandma Cuca walked to the foot of the staircase. "Bertha, come down. Rosie's here."

"I'm on the phone," Bertha called back. "I'll be there in a minute."

"Aye, que muchacha. It's my fault. I let her have the only phone in the house," Grandma Cuca said. "Sit, sit. She'll be right down, and then we'll see about a dress for you."

Rosie sat in an overstuffed chair next to a China cabinet on her left. Cuca had filled it with little ceramic figurines, ducks, dogs, farm boys, farm girls, and tiny dishes. Looking straight ahead, she studied a giant framed print of an Aztec warrior and maiden on a mountaintop that stretched upward against the wall from floor to ceiling. A deep, dark red carpet partially covered the polished wooden floor.

Turning to the right, Rosie recognized a picture she had seen before. It was Grandma Cuca's photograph when she was young and living at her family's ranch in Mexico, where she grew up. She was riding a horse, high on a ridge all alone. Her riding pants, loose at the thighs, were tucked tightly below the knee into boots. A large leather holster held a rifle whose wooden stock could be seen near her left hand. It was true. Grandma Cuca had always been able to take care of herself. She possessed a strong will, an almost supernatural streak of self-determination.

She came across the border with gold coins sewn in her petticoats and had young Quetta do the same. When she arrived in L.A., she bought a house with enough rooms to rent out. That was before her husband ran off with one of the renters and left her to care for herself and her family. But she had no problem doing it. Grandma Cuca knew how to do everything. She knew about money, property, bargaining, sewing, cooking, and people. She even had a cure for any affliction one could suffer. Her herb drinks and poultices would heal any illness; a person had only to believe in their worth for them to work.

Rosie sat there waiting and remembered the story once told to her by Grandma Cuca about Abuelita. How she left Chihuahua, Mexico, with her family after Pancho Villa's men killed her husband, destroyed her ranch, and almost burned her alive. One of Villa's men tied her to a post, doused her with kerosene, lit a match, but Pancho Villa himself stopped him. He spared her life.

"We don't burn women. Vamonos." Villa said, riding off and leaving eight-year-old Cuca to untie her mother, Abuelita.

"Rosie? Is that you?" Bertha called from the top of the stairs.

Rosie watched Bertha stroll down the stairs. Her long legs looked slim in her tight-fitting white peddle-pusher pants cinched at the waist with an extra-wide, red patent leather belt. She wore red high heel shoes and a red cotton blouse with a broad, upturned collar. She had slanted Asian eyes accented by painted black eyebrows.

"Finally, La Reina has come to join us." Grandma Cuca nodded her head toward her.

"Madre mia," Bertha said as she made her way into the living room. "Why is it always so dark in here?" She pulled back the drapes with a giant sweeping motion of her whole body. The bright sunlight caused Abuelita to abandon the rocking chair and find cover behind the curtain that hung from the entrance to her small bedroom off the living room.

"We need light to see and to live," Bertha said. "Don't you think so, Rosie?"

Rosie could only watch in wonder as Bertha ran from window to window, yanking the drapes back with violent trusts of her arms. When she had finished, she walked to the center of the room like a movie actress, bathed in white light.

"Abuelita, you can come out now," Bertha said. "I'm done."

Abuelita stuck her covered head out only long enough to squint and mumbled some words into the curtain before disappearing again.

"So, Rosie, is it true that you're going to be on television? On a game show with a bunch of boys?" Bertha took her by the hand and led her up the stairs to her bedroom. "Let's see what we can find in my closet to show you off."

In Bertha's bedroom, Rosie looked at the beautiful blonde dresser and mirror where Bertha kept her hairbrush, comb, lipstick, perfume bottles, and face powder neatly arranged on white embroidered linen. She was La Reina, the youngest child born to Grandma Cuca after coming to the United States. She always presented a mystery with her exotic eyes that no one talked about, least of all Grandma Cuca.

Rosie watched Bertha open her closet door and begin pulling out dresses on hangers one after another.

"Here's this chiffon one. I wore it only once, four years ago, for my Quinceanera. What do you think?" Bertha asked. "Too dressy, no?"

Rosie stood still, silent.

"Here's this one. I wore it for my confirmation when I was twelve." Bertha said. "No, too out of date."

Rosie said nothing.

"Come here, look in my closet. Choose whatever you want." Bertha urged. "Mama, Grandma Cuca, will make it fit. She can sew anything."

Rosie stepped to the open closet and stared at all the pretty dresses, sweaters folded on a shelf, and dozens of shoes sticking out of their boxes like Easter eggs on the floor. She <u>was</u> La Reina. Her eyes were full.

"Go on, look through them," Bertha said as she watched over Rosie's shoulder.

Rosie used her hands to move slowly through the hanging dresses. Then she found a dark brown cotton jumper with an emblem on the breast pocket embroidered with the letters "S-H." Rosie took it down and held it up against her body to see the fit.

"That? That's one of my real old Catholic school uniforms that I wore when I went to Sacred Heart Grammar School." Bertha said. "Are you sure you want this?"

"Yes, I think so," Rosie replied.

"It won't take much to alter it to fit you," Bertha said. "She'll sew it just right for you if that's what you want."

Rosie nodded.

Downstairs, Rosie took off her overalls and slipped into the jumper. She stood straight and tall on a wooden chair in the center of the living room with effort. Grandma Cuca hovered around her like a bee to a flower, adjusting the waist, folding the hem, and shortening the shoulder straps.

"Bertha, mi'ja, get me some more pins, por favor." Grandma Cuca said. "In the drawer over there."

Bertha returned with a small cushion of straight pins.

"We're almost done." Grandma Cuca said. "There, now take it off, Rosie."

Rosie carefully wiggled her body as Bertha guided the dress down to her feet, where Rosie stepped from the pool of cloth and jumped down from the chair.

"Cuidado. Aren't you the athletic one?" Bertha said, watching her bounce upright as Rosie landed on the floor.

"Rosie, mi'ja, you could hardly wait to get out of that dress." Grandma Cuca said. "Don't you like to wear pretty little dresses to school?"

Rosie shook her head from side to side with an uncomfortable "no." She pulled her overalls back on, fastening the shoulder straps with her fingers.

"Oh, give her time," Bertha said. "When the boys start to pay attention, she'll be wearing dresses to knock their eyes out."

Grandma Cuca slid the dress across the sewing machine arm, underneath the needle, and began to sew. Rosie watched from the middle of the room, not knowing what to do next.

"Come, come with me," Bertha called. "To my room where we can talk." Bertha took her by the hand and led her upstairs with excited quick steps.

"Do you have a boyfriend, Rosie?" Bertha asked as she sat on the bed and motioned with her hand for Rosie to sit next to her.

"A boyfriend? I know a lot of boys." Rosie responded, thinking of all the neighbor boys who played football with her.

"I mean a special guy. A sweetheart?" Bertha wanted to know.

Rosie shook her head, "No."

"Well, I know a lot of guys, too," Bertha said. "But only one is my special boyfriend. He's a musician. He has a band." Bertha reached over to the nightstand on her left. "Here's a picture of him. Isn't he handsome? He makes records."

Rosie smiled. Looking at the photograph, Rosie saw a brown-skinned man with black hair, black eyes, and a big smile filled with shiny white teeth. He wore a dark suit, white shirt, and tie. On the lower right corner of the photograph, he had written, "With all my love, Tosti."

"I think I want to marry him," Bertha said, taking back the picture and pressing it to her breast. "But, shhh, don't say anything to your Grandma Cuca. She doesn't like him."

Rosie gave her a promise with her eyes.

"Hey, let's go downstairs, and I'll play the record he made," Bertha said, jumping up from the bed. "It's on the radio all the time. It's called Pachuco Boogie. Come on."

Downstairs, she watched as Bertha opened the lid to the Hi-Fi stereo console, slid a record from its sleeve, and put it on the turntable.

"Here, listen to this, Rosie. You'll like the beat." Bertha said. As the lively bass backbeat began, Bertha started twisting her hips, clapping her hands, and tapping her feet to the tune. Then she kicked the rug back across the floor.

"Come on, Rosie, dance with me." Bertha grabbed her hand. "Watch me. Just do what I do."

Rosie slowly began to swing her hips and shuffle her feet when Bertha held her hands and led the way. Rosie noticed

Abuelita stick her head out from behind the curtain to watch. Grandma Cuca pulled the dress from beneath the needle and snipped the last thread as she turned to look. Now, as the boogie-woogie music filled the room, the two mothers watched their granddaughters whirl, clap, and shuffle across the polished wooden floor with smiles as big and bright as a crescent moon.

A few hours later, Rosie heard the car horn honking at the curb. Her parents had returned. Grandma put the jumper on a hanger, gave it to her as Bertha walked her out the front door to the car.

"Hi, Quetta," Bertha said as she bent down to look into the front seat. "Hi, Seve . . . Hi, how are you?"

"Rosie, did you tell her 'thank you'?" Mother asked, giving Bertha a faint smile.

"Thank you, Aunt Bertha," Rosie said as she looked up from the back seat of the car.

"Bye." Bertha waved as the car pulled away from the curb.

Rosie sensed something wrong in the car riding home but couldn't tell what it was. As she reached across the seat to hang her dress up, she was surprised by all the empty space.

"Mama, where's all the grocery bags?" Rosie asked. She stared at the back of her Mother's head that did not move. "Mama?"

"The bags are in the trunk." Mother answered, but her voice was soft and sad.

Something was wrong. Most Saturdays, there were enough grocery bags to fill both the trunk and the back seat. "But why not today?" After a few minutes, Rosie listened while her parents began to talk in Spanish about something that was stolen and how angry Dad was over the whole matter.

"El pendejo, no ve nada." Dad clenched his teeth. "Robaron todo."

Then, as the conversation got more intense, they mixed Spanish with English sentences.

"Right in front of the guy." Dad pounded his fist on the steering wheel. "El pendejo no vale por nada."

After a while, every other word was alternately Spanish, then English, until finally, Rosie heard her Dad call the parking lot attendant at Grand Central a "huevohead," and there it was-- one word was spoken, part Spanish and part English at the same time.

Rosie looked out the window from the back seat as they rode down Olympic Boulevard toward her neighborhood. She saw the Ivanwood Projects, where some of her friends lived in white stucco apartments surrounded by green shrubs and tall trees. At the corner near Soto Street, she saw kids playing caroms in front of the Lou Costello Playground and Plunge. As they drove past, Rosie looked at the empty pool that was kept unfilled through the hottest days in summer because of the polio scare. Even beaches were closed down to stop the spread of polio.

When they reached her street, Boyle Avenue, Rosie saw the huge barren lot of brown dirt with thirty-two tiny tarpaper houses that reminded her of the small wood-block houses found on a Monopoly game board. Everyone called her neighborhood the "barracks" because soldiers had trained there before they shipped out to the Pacific. After the war, returning G.I.s and their families were allowed to live there cheaply. The two-room shacks built above the ground on short wooden posts had a four-step wooden stoop that led to the front door. The main building contained communal bathrooms, showers, and laundry. At the center of the lot was a giant incinerator where everyone put his trash. The heavy cast iron door squealed on rusted hinges when it opened, and the "clank" of the crossbar when it closed was a familiar sound in the neighborhood.

Dad pulled up to the front door stoop and parked the car, then went inside the house. Rosie got out of the car with her dress on a hanger and circled to the trunk. To her surprise, Rosie watched Mother step from the car and walk up the front steps.

"Mama, the bags, the groceries," Rosie called. "I can help carry them in."

"Mi'ja, come inside." Mother said. "There are no groceries."

"What?" Rosie went toward her Mother.

"All the groceries were stolen from the car when it was in the parking lot." Mother said. "Don't worry about it, mi'ja. Some things can't be helped."

Right then, Rosie knew there would be little to eat this coming week and no lunches for school. Rosie knew how it would be. There wasn't food in the house many times because Dad would blow his whole paycheck at Tiny's Bar on a Friday night.

"Tienes que ser fuerte." Mother counseled. "Going without lunch, you'll learn to be strong. Como las puras mujeres."

Chapter Three

They approached the parking lot at the south entrance of County Hospital, where Irma was a patient in the polio ward. Then Rosie noticed some men wearing white and blue striped pajamas wandering around in a patio area surrounded by a chain-link fence topped with barbed wire. A tall skinny man with messy black hair and leché-white skin seemed to be turning slowly in a tight circle and talking to himself.

"Mom, who are they? What are they doing at the hospital?" Rosie asked, unable to take her eyes from the strange sight.

"Rosie, don't stare at them." Mother said. "Look the other way. Those men have troubles."

"Troubles?" Rosie asked. "What kind of troubles?"

"You ask too many questions." Dad broke in. "Do what your Mother asked. Look the other way. Those guys are a little touched here." Dad tapped his index finger to the side of his head.

"What does that mean? Touched?" Rosie asked.

"Rosie, mi'ja, those guys are crazy. You know, loco." Dad spoke. "Every hospital has a ward for the insane. That's them."

"Oh." Rosie continued to stare.

"Here, listen to this." Dad began to tell a story. "There's a guy driving by the insane asylum when he gets a flat tire. He stops at the curb and starts to change his tire. Well, all the locos come and stand by the fence to watch him. It makes the guy nervous, but he figures they're behind the fence and can't hurt him. But he's nervous anyway and tips the hubcap over where he put all the wheel lug nuts, and they roll into the sewer hole. 'Oh, damn, he says, what am I going to do now? How am I going to put the spare tire back on without the lug nuts?'

'I know what you can do to get that spare tire on.' Says a voice from behind him.

The guy turns around, and it's one of the locos, with a strange smile on his face, talking to him through the fence. 'What? Mind your own business. Ok.'

'Look, friend, I can help you.' The loco says. 'Take one lug nut off each of the other tires, and you'll have three that you can use to tightened the spare back on until you can get to a gas station to get more lug nuts to replace the ones you lost.'

The guy scratches his head and thinks, 'That's not a bad idea.' So, he does it, and it works. So, he says to the loco who's been watching all the time. 'Hey, thanks a lot for that great idea. But can I ask you something? Why are you in *there* if you can think smart like that?'

And the loco says, 'No one ever said I was stupid, just crazy.'

Dad had a big grin on his face at the end of the story, and so did Mother. Still, Rosie just sat there in the back seat, trying to understand the difference between stupid and crazy.

****

After parking the car, Dad led the way to the elevator that took them to the third floor, the polio ward.

Standing by the examination table, Rosie held Irma's hand as Irma lay on her back. Rosie noticed Irma's extended right leg, encased in a white dinghy plaster, scribbled well wishes, names, slogans, and cartoon drawings of Popeye and Daffy Duck.

"Will she be coming home soon?" Dad asked, looking uneasy in the sterling hospital light, probably because of the doctor's superior manner.

"Soon." Doctor Mesmer responded. "You do realize that Irma was very fortunate that only the hamstring muscle in the right leg was affected. She has some weakness there now that may be permanent. It depends. But the paralysis has subsided. The new cast will help." Doctor Mesmer paused. "She'll be home soon, and this time to stay."

As Rosie watched her Mother and Dad smile at one another, and their eyes welled up with tears, she remembered that once before Dad had asked the doctor, "Why my daughter?"

And Doctor Mesmer had responded, "There are many theories, but we really don't know why some children are stricken, and others are not."

Rosie put her hand to her Santa Maria medal and prayed as the doctor's voice drew back her attention.

"Go to the nurse's station now to complete and sign some paperwork while I change Irma's cast." Doctor Mesmer said as he adjusted the wire-rim glasses on his nose.

"Can Rosie stay?" Irma asked, showing fake sad eyes Rosie had seen her use many times before.

"Yes, that will be fine." Doctor Mesmer smiled. After caring for Irma for over twelve months, he knew she possessed the feminine guile not usually found in one so young.

"It won't hurt." Doctor Mesmer assured. "Don't let the buzzing noise scare you." He began cutting open her leg cast at the upper end near her thigh. As he moved down her leg, the vibrating round blade cut a thin slit down to her foot. "Now, the other side." He began cutting down the inside length of her leg.

"Now, that's it." Doctor Mesmer said as he lifted the sliced cast like a halved avocado from its pit. But, as he did, spoons, forks, and a butter knife fell out, rattling and clattering to the white linoleum floor like sleigh bells in the school Christmas assembly.

"My word, where did all this come from?" Doctor Mesmer asked. "I'm sure the cafeteria will be glad to get these back."

An "I don't know" look crossed Irma's face as Rosie watched her hold back a smile.

"Now, Irma . . ." Doctor Mesmer said.

"It just itches so much, doctor," Irma said. "Can you do anything about that, the itching?"

"We'll see." Doctor Mesmer said. He removed the bottom half of the cast and began to examine the feeble leg, wrinkled and shriveled like a long green chili. "Hmmm." The Doctor walked his fingers along her thigh muscles and down to her calf, finally the ankle and foot.

"Does this hurt?" Doctor Mesmer said as he pressed his fingertips along a nine-inch scar that ran from her ankle up along the calf muscle, ending just below the back of the knee. He had explained before that he had to cut the sinew to relieve the tension and pain, breaking the poliovirus's grip.

"No, no, it doesn't, but, but, "Irma hesitated. Rosie looked on without saying a word.

"I know, I know," The Doctor said. "The scar. But guess what, most of it will be hidden by the bobby socks you'll wear when you go dancing. Isn't that right, Rosie?"

Rosie half-smiled at the doctor and then looked away. She thought about how she had just learned to dance with Aunt Bertha at Grandma Cuca's house.

"Oh, she don't dance," Irma said. "Just me. I can show you right now. Wanna see?"

"That's okay. I believe you." The doctor held her down with his hand on her shoulder. "Well, it is looking pretty good, but we still need to work on the right foot."

"What's wrong with it?" Irma asked, inviting the doctor to reveal what she very well knew already.

Rosie cracked her knuckles and tossed her ponytail back over her shoulder.

"Look here. It points to the south when it should point to the north." The doctor answered as he tugged lightly at her toes. "But instead of the entire leg being immobilized, you'll only need a partial cast that will come to here, just below the knee."

"Hey, Rosie," Irma said. "Now, I can wear wool skirts I always wanted and not look funny."

Rosie watched as the doctor and nurse prepared a new cast that covered Irma's entire foot except for her toes that were sticking out like a bunch of pink grapes.

"After it dries, don't walk on it until we get some new, better crutches. These old sticks need to be replaced." Doctor Mesmer handed the wooden crutches to the nurse, and they both walked out of the room.

When the cast was dry, Rosie helped Irma into a wheelchair.

"Let's get out of here," Irma said. "Let's go do something fun."

Rosie pushed her out of the examination room and down the hallway toward her ward bed.

"I need to go to the restroom. Will you help me?" Irma pointed in the direction of the women's restroom.

Once inside, Irma looked into the mirror, lifting herself from the worn wheelchair. "Marilyn Monroe?" Irma asked. "Did he say I looked like Marilyn Monroe?

"I think Doctor Mesmer said Liz Taylor," Rosie answered into the mirror. "You've got green eyes, pretty eyes like she does."

"Look in my bag and get me an eyebrow pencil so I can put that mole right there at the corner of my mouth," Irma said. She used her left forearm to balance herself on the sink while she pointed the pencil's sharpened end right next to the corner of her mouth. The weight of her leg pulled her back down into the chair as the pencil drew downward at her chin. "Oh, damn."

"I'll do it for you." Rosie spat into a tissue and wiped Irma's chin. Then Rosie got face to face with Irma and aimed the pencil point at the corner of Irma's mouth. "There, look, just like her, Liz Taylor. Look in the mirror."

Irma edged up from the wheelchair and saw her narrow face lighted by green eyes and a small black dot at the corner of her mouth, as alive as a musical note on school chart paper.

"Now, let's go down to look at the dead bodies." Irma clutched the chair's wheels and pushed forward, sending herself out of the restroom into the hallway.

"Wait, Irma," Rosie called. "How are we going to get in the elevator to go down there? You told me that it's off-limits. Besides your friend, the guy that watches the door won't let us take the elevator to the morgue."

"You're right, he won't let <u>us</u>, but he'd do anything for Liz Taylor. You'll see."

Just as Irma hit the elevator button to go down, Rosie heard a male voice from behind.

"Ladies, where do you think you're going?"

Rose turned Irma in the chair to face him. The voice belonged to a young orderly.

"Irma, oh, pardon me, Miss Taylor, you know you can't go down there. Liz, this is your floor."

"Ah, com' on, Jaime, please," Irma said as she turned to face him. "Look, this is my younger sister, and she's bored up here. Com' on. We want to ride the elevator up and down a couple of times f just for the fun of it."

Rosie looked at Jaime with a shy smile and turned away. For her, meeting new people was like sticking your toes into ice-cold water.

"Ah, all right, but hurry right back before anybody misses you." Jaime helped push the wheelchair into the elevator. "Right back, now. Don't get me in trouble."

"We won't." Irma smiled as the doors pulled together, and the elevator moved slowly downward.

"What's really down there?" Rosie brushed back her ponytail and leaned forward to look into Irma's eyes for the truth, which was hard to do because Irma had a way with her eyes — she made them show you whatever you wanted to see.

"Oh, lots of weird stuff," Irma said. "I've heard the nurses and the doctors talk about brains, hands, and feet in jars like pickles."

"Like pickles? For reals, Irma?" Rosie asked, squeezing the wheelchair handles while her heart jumped to her throat.

"That's what I heard them say," Irma answered. "Even babies." Irma gave up those two words like a murmur before a scream.

"What?" Rosie moved in front of Irma to search her entire face. "Irma?"

"You know, little, tiny babies that die before they're even born," Irma responded.

"For reals?" Rosie felt the elevator come to a stop as the doors slowly opened into a long dark hallway. "Are you sure you want to do this?"

"Sure, aren't you?" Irma asked. "Com' on, we'll just check it out for a little while."

Rosie slowly pushed the wheelchair along the corridor until they reached a set of double doors with windows.

"Look in there, Rosie," Irma said. "Tell me what you see."

Rosie pushed the wheelchair as close as she could to the doors and used the handles to lift herself to look through one of the small windows.

"What do you see? What do you see?"

Her arms strained beneath her weight as Rosie stretched her body to get a good view.

"Nothing. It's too dark inside." Rosie replied. "Let's try another one down the hall."

Rosie pushed Irma along until we approached another double door entrance.

"There's light coming out of the door window," Irma said. "Try looking into that one."

Rosie supported herself with her hands clasped to the wheelchair handles. She stretched her arms rigid, holding her up to the small rectangular window.

"I see some people in there, nurses and a doctor standing next to a metal table."

"What are they doing?" Irma asked.

"I don't know," Rosie looked around until her eyes caught sight of a shelf lined with big jars filled with yellow liquid and strange floating stuff she couldn't quite figure out. Then, as Rosie began to lower herself down, she recognized the shape of a, a, - - - no it couldn't be, her breath escaped as she dropped to her feet, landing hard on the floor.

"What happened? What did you see?" Irma asked.

"I thought I saw ah, ah, ah . . ." Rosie couldn't get her breath. "I don't know.'

"Com' on, Rosie, help me up. Rosie, help me up. I wanna see." Irma said.

Rosie helped Irma out of the chair and held it firm while Irma leaned against it for balance and stretched her body to look in.

"It looks like a baby," Irma whispered.

"Hey, girls." A deep male voice called from behind us. "What are you doing down here."

Irma collapsed back into the chair. Then Rosie wheeled it around to face the voice belonging to a young man probably in his thirties in a green gown and a green mask strung about his neck.

"You two shouldn't be down here." He called out. "No one's allowed down here."

"We're lost," Irma said. "Please help us to get out of here." Irma began to cry. "We were trying to get to the cafeteria to get something to eat."

"O.K., O.K., don't cry." He said. "Just get back into the elevator and go to the 6th floor. That's where the cafeteria is. Now go."

"Thanks, mister." Irma sobbed a little as Rosie rolled her down the hall to the elevator.

Once they were inside the elevator and the doors closed, Rosie let go of a big breath.

"Oh, I was so scared. Me asusto when he called out to us."

"I wasn't scared, but I think I saw what you did," Irma said. "I only started crying because it always works, especially with men."

"What works?" Rosie asked.

"You know when you're in trouble or want something. Just cry a little, and a man will always feel sorry for you."

Rosie watched the elevator doors open like curtains to Irma's floor.

"Let's stay out here and watch people go by," Irma said. But after a while, with nothing to do, Irma grew restless. "Let's go see my friend."

"What friend?" Rosie asked.

"He's down the hall, in the next ward. He's got polio too. But real bad, but don't stare at him, okay." Irma said.

"He can't walk?" Rosie asked, pushing Irma along down the hallway.

"Mira Mirror, that's what Jose and the other kids call him, but his name is Chris," Irma said.

"Mira Mirror? Why? What's wrong with him?" Rosie asked.

"You'll see," Irma said. He's got a terrible case of polio. Here, turn here, into this room." Irma called.

As Rosie steered the wheelchair to the right, Irma motioned with her hand to keep pushing down an aisle with five or six beds on each side until they came in sight of a large machine standing against a wall. Like a shiny container on its side, a large steel tube was supported by thin metal legs with wheels at the ends. The dull off-white metal barrel had shiny glass porthole windows and black knobs on its surface. At the top, three or four windows of various sizes were cut into the sides and framed in stainless steel, held in place with chrome bolts. The machine made a low continuous hum that droned in her ears as Rosie drew closer with Irma in the wheelchair.

"What's that?" Rosie asked.

"That's my friend Chris," Irma said. "That's his iron lung. He's inside so he can breathe."

Rosie came within a foot of the machine she had never seen before. Her eyes tried to take everything in, the metal, the glass, and the bolts. Then without warning, Rosie realized that at one end of the tube was a boy's tiny head, sticking out, face-up, looking into a slanted glass mirror about six inches above him.

"Hi, Irma." The head spoke. "Move over and closer a bit so I can see you better."

When Rosie didn't respond, Irma grabbed the wheels and moved forward. Rosie lost her balance and steadied herself with one hand against the steel tube. It was cold.

"Hey, Chris," said Irma. "Meet my sister, Rosie. Rosie, this is Chris."

"Hi, Rosie," Chris spoke to the image in the mirror above his head that let him view the two of them, smiling just a few inches away.

He had freckles on the cheeks of his thin face and a patch of reddish-brown hair. His eyes were brown and bright.

Rosie was confused and unable to speak, having never seen anything like this before.

"Hey, Rosie," Chris called. "I bet you don't know who's the best wheelchair racer on this floor or maybe the whole hospital."

"What? Who?" Rosie felt her heart pound as Irma's elbow nudged her.

"Your sister, Irma," Chris said. "When no one's around, she sets up races, right here in her ward."

"Races? Really, Irma?" Rosie looked at Irma, who was smiling into the mirror at Chris.

"Yeah, and she's the best and the fastest. She'll beat anybody, even the nurses and helpers. On two wheels, imagine." "Irma, be careful, cuidado." Rosie reached for the wheelchair handles as Irma shifted her weight back and held the front wheels off the floor, like a stallion rearing on its hind legs. "Oh, don't worry about her." Chris smiled. "She won't fall. She never falls."

"Well, maybe once." Irma laughed.

"From here I can't see everything, but I can sure hear it all. The rubber wheels running across the floor, the sweaty hands grabbing the spinning spokes, the shouts, and laughs. Mostly the laughs. I love that. Huh, Irma."

"That's right, Chris," Irma replied. "And one day soon you'll be out here racing with us."

"You think so?" Chris asked.

"I know so?" Irma said. "Hey, here comes your nurse. We'd better go now before she kicks us out. Bye, Chris."

"Bye, Irma. Bye, Rosie." Chris said, smiling into the mirror. "And thanks for coming over."

"Bye, Chris," Rosie said to the lively, freckled face in the mirror.

****

Rosie sat in a chair along the corridor wall next to Irma. Then without a word, Irma placed her hands in the air to invite Rosie to play patty-cake. As they clapped hands together, they began to recite, "Rover, rover . . ."

When Rosie missed the beat, they both laughed and sighed.

"Irma, I'm going to be on the Hail the Champ show," Rosie said.

"Oh, Rosie, on TV?"

Rosie nodded yes.

"Gees, I wish I could go with you."

"Dad says we might be able to bring you home by then, so you can watch on TV with Robert," Rosie said.

"When, when, when is it?"

"Only a few weeks away."

"I'll be okay by then," Irma said. "I'll be home, running in the middle of the street like we used to, kicking the chancla meada under the street lights with the boys chasing us.

"Yeah, that will be fun," Rosie said. "And maybe you can ride the bike if I win it."

"Oh, Rosie, you'll win it," Irma said. "You'll win everything. Just wait and see."

Chapter Four

On Monday morning, Rosie awoke from a bad dream—a dream about losing something. She stretched out her arms and legs beyond the limits of her cotton pajamas. Then Rosie yawned, sucking in a short quick breath, and put the tips of her fingers to her throat, expecting to find her Santa Maria medal there, but it wasn't. Rosie jumped out of bed and searched under the covers with her hands. Nothing. She threw the cotton cover on the floor and lifted the pillow into the air. Still nothing. How could this be? Buttons get lost from sweaters; baseballs get lost in sewer drains. Kites get lost in tree branches. But her medal? Rosie remembered she had it on while she prayed, kneeling beside her bed before sleeping. Lost in the night? It wasn't really happening. It wasn't . . . .

"Mama, mama," Rosie called, crushing the pillow to her chest and burying her face in it.

"What, what's wrong," Mother hurried into her room.

"I lost my Santa Maria," Rosie whispered.

"Where?"

"I don't know. It was around my neck when I went to bed last night." Rosie explained. "But now, it's gone."

"Rosie, mi'ja," Mother stroked her hair. "Don't worry. I'll find it. You get ready for school."

****

At Wilson Junior High playground, Rosie sat on a long wooden bench, waiting for her turn to play tetherball. She watched two seventh-grade girls swing and punch the white rubber ball until, without warning, the rope broke loose, and the ball flew at her. She heard some girls shriek and watched the ball land at her feet like a wounded bird with a scraggly tail. When Rosie bent over to pick it up, her hands reached forward, but her eyes saw nothing but darkness as the memory of the day Irma got polio came alive, like a movie in her head.

It was noon recess on a gray Friday, and Irma had beaten everyone who had challenged her to a game of tetherball.

So, now, Lucha, whose real name was Lucia, but everybody called her Lucha because she liked to fight a lot—with girls and boys. It didn't matter which. She just wanted to fight, and she liked to win. Rosie had heard all the stories about Lucha's mother being a curandera and how even Lucha had some magic powers, too.

Lucha didn't play tetherball much, but Rosie figured Lucha wasn't going to let Irma be the champ in tetherball without having a go at it first.

With the ball in one hand, Lucha made a tight fist with the other, and bang, hit the ball so hard it went around three times above Irma's head, out of reach. Then, Lucha ran to one side and slapped at the ball as it passed through her side of the circle, arching the ball into the air over Irma's head and back into her own hands.

Irma jumped, stretched, and reached with both hands above her head but couldn't stop the ball from circling above. All the kids on the playground had gathered around, some shouting for Irma and others for Lucha. Irma watched the rope wind tighter and tighter around the pole. Then she did something nobody expected, least of all, Lucha. Irma deserted her spot, ran to the centerline right next to Lucha, and raised her hands to block the ball. Lucha tried to slap at it as it came around. The ball made a loud popping sound against Irma's upraised hands and rebounded back, behind Lucha to the opposite side. Both girls ran after it, being careful not to cross the centerline.

Irma grabbed it away from Lucha's reach. She began belting the ball around, unwinding the rope in Lucha's direction and rewinding it to her advantage. The crowd of kids grew closer to watch, and the cheering grew louder as Irma swatted the white rubber ball around and around as Lucha leaped and stretched her arms into the air helplessly. Now the end was near. Irma continued to wind the rope tightly, drawing both girls closer to the pole.

Only a foot of rope remained; the ball was in Irma's hands. She held it aloft in her left hand and punched it with all her might, sending it across toward Lucha. Lucha leaped high, swinging her fist, blocking the ball, and sending it back toward Irma, who was caught off balance. Irma reached for the wobbly slow-moving ball, but as it touched her hands, she fell to the ground, landing on her back. She turned on her side and tried to get up, but her legs were as rigid as broomsticks. Lucha seized the ball and began to fling it around and around, unwinding the rope.

"Get up, Irma, get up." A gang of shrill voices shouted.

Irma used her arms to lift the upper half of her body from the ground, but her legs remained cramped, stiff with pain, and did not move. She tried to get up again and again, but her legs did not get under her.

As if stuck to the blacktop, Irma looked around at all the screaming faces until she found Rosie's scared eyes. Then Irma reached out her hand, and Rosie ran to her, knelt beside her.

"What's wrong? Are you all right?" Rosie cradled Irma's head in her lap as the yard duty teacher waded through the excited crowd and blew her silver whistle for help.

The memory evaporated when Rosie heard a freckled-faced girl asking, "Can we have our ball back, can we?" Rosie handed the ball to the young girl just as the bell rang to end recess.

Since that day, when Irma fell and couldn't get up, Rosie wondered if Lucha used the powers of a curandera to cast a spell on Irma to win the game.

****

Rosie sat in the front row of the class, close to the teacher's desk because she liked to smell the fresh-cut flowers the Miss Glass always brought from her garden to place on the corner of her desk. Rosie watched Miss Glass as she stood in front of the chalkboard, her hands clasped together in front of her, her feet planted firmly, and her head erect. She was wearing a light blue dress with a freshly ironed white collar. Rosie looked from the teacher's stature to the vase of small violet flower petals and back again, thinking how much they were the same-- pretty, bright, soft, and fragrant.

"Who has a March of Dimes card today?" Miss Glass asked, standing next to her desk arranged with books, pens in a coffee cup, an in/out basket, a datebook, and a crystal vase of flowers.

Rosie walked to the front of the room and handed the worn card filled with twelve Roosevelt dimes.

"Rosie, that's wonderful." Miss Glass said. The teacher put a rubber band around the small stack of cards she held in her hand. "You know, students, your contributions are going to help find a cure for polio someday. Right now, a vaccine, a shot of medicine, is being studied by Doctor Salk, who is funded by all these dimes that all of you are donating."

"A cure?" Rosie asked as she sat down at her desk. "Will it help people who have it now get better? Will it help my sister?"

"Rosie, that's a good question." Miss Glass responded. "But right now, I believe, Doctor Salk is trying to find a vaccine to prevent someone from getting polio, not curing someone who has it already."

"Does anybody have a cure?" Rosie asked, focusing her eyes on the teacher's face.

"Well, I don't think so." Miss Glass continued. "But I have read about a woman named Sister Kenny. She's a nurse who treats polio patients, many of whom show great improvement and walk again after being stricken with polio."

Rosie turned away. She was not sure if a nun could help her family, help Irma.

****

Later at home, Rosie thought about Irma at the hospital. Rosie imagined her sitting in a wheelchair month after month, her leg in a cast, waiting to come home. Rosie felt sad about all the days she had missed having her sister home to be with, playing hop-scotch, jumping rope, and kicking the chancla meada. But at that moment, Rosie closed her eyes, clasped her hands, and prayed that her sister would get well and come home soon.

"Rosie, look what I found," Mother said as she walked into the bedroom with the Santa Maria's medal dangling from a thin chain.

"Oh, momma," Rosie stood up and reached for it. "You found it. You found it."

"Mira, let me have it, and I'll put it on you." Mother turned her around by the shoulders. "The clasp was broken, but I fixed it. There, let me see. Que bonita."

Rosie hugged her Mother with both arms wrapped around her waist.

****

Robert got off work at five. Rosie waited for him in their room and played with her yo-yo, practicing the "baby's cradle" and "walking the dog." She heard her Mother and Dad laughing through the thin wall. Rosie took a peek into the other room to see what was so funny. She saw Mother chasing flies out of the house with a dish towel and Dad looking in the cupboards to check the liquor supply before he headed out to the Second Street Liquor store. Rosie knew the routine. It was Saturday. Dad would give her and Robert money to go to the show, and her parents would invite their friends and relatives over for a "get together." They never called it a party because it was family and friends getting together for no reason at all, or maybe the best reason, which is no reason.

Rosie knew what the get-together would be like. When she was younger, too young to go to the show on Saturday nights, aunts, uncles, friends, and neighbors would start arriving with brown paper bags that went straight to the cupboard. Soon all the women were in the kitchen talking and laughing while the men were sitting at the table playing cards, smoking, and drinking like their lives depended on it. The old Mexican songs played in the background with lyrics about an unfair life, undeserved love, and undying remorse.

Rosie recalled just such a night when the men, or maybe the women, began to argue about who could make the hottest chili salsa. Arms firmly crossed beneath her breasts, Aunt Ruth claimed she had the hottest recipe. Uncle Joe argued that he positively knew who had the hottest salsa in all of East L.A. It was his wife, Letti. Finally, someone said, "Put your money where your mouth is." And just like that, the women went home, got their ingredients, returned to her house, and started chopping, grating, heating, peeling, and mashing chilies of every shape and size. They wanted to make the hottest chili salsa to make their husbands proud.

"Hoye, here's the deal," Manny said. "We're going to find out who makes the hottest chili salsa in all of East L.A., or maybe all of California tonight, once and for all. Any man who wants to taste and judge the chili that the women prepare must sit at the table and eat. There will be no water, bread, and nothing to soothe the "picada." If you leave the table, the chili is too hot for you, and you're out! The last man will eat the hottest chili until he, too, can't stand it anymore and quits. But then we'll know who makes the hottest chili in the world; that bowl of fire will sit on the table, solito, the proof of one woman's curse upon all men."

So, it went late into the night, with their women proudly bringing their hottest mix in their favorite wooden, clay, or chiseled stone bowl, a molcajete, to the table for the eager men. They sat poised, wooden spoon in hand, ready for molten lava that would leave taste buds sizzling on their tongue like drops of water on a hot cast iron placa. As the night wore on, brave uncles and dear friends left the table in embarrassing ways. After eating Aunt Refugio's chili that she swore handed down from the Aztecas, Uncle Tomas's face turned as red as a tin-can beach sunburn in July. His body seemed to melt from his chair down to the floor beneath the table where he stayed for quite a while, forgotten by the others. Later, after Big Al ate a spoonful of Aunt Licha's chili guerito especiale, he jumped to his feet, knocking his chair to the floor behind him, stared out at nothingness, and blew hot air thru his nose. He ran around the table five times before he collapsed into someone else's vacant chair and announced, "I'm still alive." Meaning he was still in the chili contest.

But he was thrown out anyway. Rules were rules. He left the table. The contest went on into the night. And as the chili got hotter and the tasters got fewer. At 2 a.m., Grandma Cuca's recipe, prepared by Rosie's Mother, habaneras ground in a molcajete, proved to be the undoing of everyman and the pride of the party's host.

But this Saturday night, Rosie was going to the show with Robert to see an old movie at the R-K-O on Brooklyn Avenue. The film's name was "Sister Kenny," with Rosalind Russell starring in the leading role. When Robert arrived, he came into the house whistling a tune, pulled back the curtain, and threw his rolled-up apron on his bed.

"Hey, let's go," Robert said to Rosie. "Mundo and the guys are going to meet us there."

The RKO marquee stuck out from the building like a wedge of cake decorated with colorful neon icing. Rosie waited in line at the door while Robert bought the tickets with his own money. Once inside, Robert paid for a bag of popcorn and some jujubes for Rosie.

"Hey, Mundo, lay off," Robert said without turning around when he felt an arm lock around his neck. "Rosie, I'll see you later. Where you gonna be? Oh, I know, upfront, right?"

Rosie nodded yes. She took the popcorn and candy in hand. She walked away across the carpet, leaving Robert and

Mundo play-boxing and eyeballing some girls who just walked into the theater.

Rosie followed the footlights down to the first row, in front, next to the stage. She sat at about the middle of the row, sitting her bottom on a folded seat until it clanked open and scooped her in. Here the upholstered chairs still had fabric on them, and Rosie didn't have to worry about a sharp wire spring poking her skin. She missed not having Irma with her.

Once the projector flashed its cone of light, the red velvet curtain, like magic wings, parted to each side, uncovering a white landscape with freckled light racing across it for an instant. Then an image of a steel lattice radio tower sparked the letters R-K-O.

When sitting this close, Rosie, head tilted up, loved the feeling of being in the movie, surrounded by the actors and having to look from one face to another as they spoke. When Rosalind Russell appeared in her starched nurse's uniform, Rosie scanned the beautiful dark-haired figure from head to foot by slowly tilting her head, looking from the tip of the nurse's spotless white hat down to her polished white leather shoes. It was like being there. In-person. In the movie.

After a while, Rosie heard giggling and muffled voices to her left. It was Lucha in a tight red sweater, coming down the aisle with her friends to walk across in front of the screen just to make a scene and let all the boys know she was there. When Lucha passed, she gave Rosie a hard look and elbowed her friend, like saying, "Look who's here, Irma's sister." Rosie stared back but was afraid. She touched her Santa Maria medal through her overall bib. After they left, Rosie looked to the back of the theater, hoping to see Robert there. He wasn't. He probably was in the bathroom, smoking with Mundo and the guys or making time with some girls in the lobby.

Rosie soon forgot about Lucha and everybody else. She just sat there staring at the screen. She finished her popcorn and sucked on jujubes that stuck to her teeth.

Then, as she watched, one scene gripped her: in a hospital, doctors surround Sister Kenny in a big room with windows all around for people to look through. Doctors stare at Sister Kenny like they want to catch her making a mistake or saying something wrong.

But Sister Kenny works her hands on the legs of a little girl who has polio as the doctors shake their heads in disgust. They argue with her, but Sister Kenny stands strong and isn't afraid of these doctors who think they know it all because they went to college, and Sister Kenny has only nurse's training. But she doesn't back down. She knows she is right.

And by the movie's end, everyone agreed Sister Kenny was right and the children crippled with polio walked again. When the show ended, many people clapped, but Rosie sat still, as if in prayer, until the lights brightened. Then she got up and headed for the lobby where Robert would meet her. As she reached the exit at the end of the steep aisle, she saw Lucha and her gang of girls waiting for her. Rosie thought about walking back and finding another way out, but she knew they would think she was "chicken." So, she continued in their direction, not knowing when they would make their move. As Rosie drew near, Lucha stepped in front of her, blocking her way. Rosie clenched her hands at her sides and looked into Lucha's steely eyes. Lucha raised a tight fist.

"Com' on, sis, let's go," Robert said, stepping in and putting his arm around Rosie's shoulders. "And tell me about the movie, so if anyone asks, I'll know what to say."

Rosie moved past Lucha and her gang like she didn't even notice them.

****

Outside, the boys talked in hushed tones as Rosie walked a few steps behind them toward home. She was quiet and deep in thought. She wondered why they acted so differently at the show. Was it the girls? She couldn't understand why they had to joke around so much when the girls were nearby and why they seem to light up like Roman Candles on the Fourth of July if a girl even looked at them, let alone smiled.

And what about the girls who were smiling with shiny white teeth like neon lights on the theater marquee. Irma called it flirting. It's just for fun, she had said. Try it. Irma had all the right moves, the looks, and the eyes. Rosie remembered the time Irma came home from school with her eyebrows shaved off and replaced with a thin dark line from an eyebrow pencil. She thought Mother and Dad wouldn't notice. She cried when Mother grabbed her by the shoulders and said, "Irma, what have you done? Mira, no mas. Just wait till your Dad comes home and sees you."

But Irma knew she had little to worry about. She was Dad's favorite, and besides, he would have no choice but to let her draw the black pencil line above her eye until her eyebrow grew back in.

When Rosie asked, "Irma, why did you do it?"

Irma winked and replied, "'Cause the boys like it."

Rosie wondered if she would ever care enough about what the boys liked to shave her eyebrows off for them.

Chapter Five

Rosie woke up to the loud rapping at her bedroom window. She looked across the small room toward the window and noticed that Robert was not in his bed. The playful knocking continued. Who could it be? She went to the window, drew the curtain back, and saw Robert and Mundo grinning and fanning their hands for her to come outside into the backyard.

"What'd you want?" Rosie asked as she approached the boys. "Robert, don't you have work today?" Rosie waited for an answer, but the boys just laughed and motioned with their hands for her to look behind them. When she did, she saw about five car tires placed on the ground, black circles on the dirt.

"Rosie, do you think you can run through them?" Robert asked. "You know this is one of the tests on the show, and you have to beat the other guy. Right, Mundo.

"That's right," Mundo said. "I saw them do it the other night on TV, on Hail the Champ."

"We thought you should practice so you can win," Robert said. "Look, I'll show you what to do. Com' on Mundo." Robert crouched down to ready himself for the sprint across the tires. Robert pranced in and out of all five tires with a high-stepping stride as he ran at top speed. Behind him was Mundo, but Mundo tumbled to the ground with one faulty step, grabbing his ankle in pain.

"But don't do it like me," Mundo called to Rosie. "Now you try it."

"Go on. You can do it." Robert said. "Rosie, run as fast as you can without falling like I did."

Rose stared down the row of tires, leaned forward on the balls of her feet, and dashed off. She imitated the high-stepping stride of her brother as she sped in and out of one tire, then another to the end.

"That's it. You did better than me." Mundo said.

"That's my sis," Robert said. "Not too bad. Try it again, this time faster."

Rosie took a deep breath and charged off again, thinking how much easier this was than a fast game of hop-scotch with the girls.

"Way to go!" Robert said as Rosie finished her second run without falling. "Now, keep practicing. Mundo and me will help you, but right now, I got to go to work."

Rosie nodded her head and readied herself to charge forward again. Mundo kicked the tires before giving Rosie the signal to go headlong through the course without tripping.

****

Before the end of the school day on Monday, Mother Superior and Miss Donna, the lay teacher, came to Rosie's room and asked for the children attending catechism that day. Several of the girls were preparing for their confirmation at the Los Flores Catholic Church. Rosie was one of them. Mother Superior went from room to room until she had gathered all her students and led them out the front of the school down the street toward the church on Soto Avenue. First, she would ask certain girls to be at the head of the line and others to follow at the end. Rosie didn't understand why some girls were chosen over others to lead the two lines of girls walking down the street. But after a while, she realized that Mother Superior was making a point – the girls wearing dresses have the special privilege of being first. The others, like Rosie, who wore jeans or bib overalls, Mother Superior assigned to the back of the line. Mother Superior often scolded, "When boys begin wearing dresses, girls can wear pants, but not until then." They all knew that a stare from her atomic eyes would melt skin like the candle wax on the altar.

When they arrived at the church entrance, each girl dipped two fingers into the basin of holy water and made the sign of the cross. They walked down the center aisle with their heads bowed and covered toward the front and genuflected before entering the pew where they sat, ready to begin their lessons. Miss Donna always started with a short prayer asking for blessings for the young girls—that their hearts and minds would be open to the instruction given.

Rosie liked her teacher. Dressed in a loose-fitting dress that hung from her narrow shoulders, Miss Donna, about twenty-three years old, looked much older than she was. She had a sensitive and caring manner with the girls. And Rosie noticed that her voice was unusual, unique. Whenever she said "God," the word came from her lips slowly and from someplace deep down, like a pail drawn up from a dark well. She often told cautionary tales about her youth or enlightened the girls about newsworthy events of the day.

Now Miss Donna's voice brought Rosie back from her reverie to the church's confines and the image of Miss Donna standing in front of her.

"Today, the reward for the best student will be this," Miss Donna held up a large coin. "It's a fifty-cent piece I found on the sidewalk on the way here. I think it's a lucky sign, and I want one of you to have it."

"Ooooh," all the girls uttered at once. Fifty cents could buy many wonderful things at Ramos market – a hairbrush, berets with rhinestones, necklaces made of candy beads, and silver rings made of plastic and enough change left over for a Nesbitt orange drink, too.

Rosie noticed Cece, a skinny girl, a friend of Lucha, stare at the coin like she had never seen one before and maybe she hadn't. Rosie caught Cece's eyes then turned away. She didn't need any more trouble with Lucha and her gang.

Rosie knew exactly what she would do if she won the coin, so she raised her hand to recite prayers, the Ten Commandments, and the Seven Sacraments from memory. Miss Donna asked Rosie to come to the altar and stand next to her at the hour's end.

"Rosie," Miss Donna began. "You have studied and remembered all the essential things that are required to be eligible for Confirmation. And today I'm selecting you to receive the prize. She placed the silver coin into Rosie's hand. The girls clapped, but Rosie stood still and said nothing.

"Is something wrong?" Miss Donna bent down to look into Rosie's eyes.

"Thank you, Miss Donna," Rosie replied. "But, could I have five dimes for this?" She handed the coin back to Miss Donna.

"I think so," Miss Donna went to her coin purse. "Here, Rosie, five dimes."

Rosie smiled as she looked down at the small silver Roosevelt coins in her hand.

****

Later that evening at home, Rosie sat on her bed reading a book when her Mother came into the room with tears in her eyes.

"Rosie, put your shoes on." Mother said. "We're going to the hospital. It's Irma."

"Irma? What's wrong, mama?" Rosie searched her Mother's face for an answer. "Mama?"

"Nothing. I mean, Irma's all right." Mother said. "It's just that she's upset, upset about Chris, her friend at the hospital."

"What happened?" Rosie asked. "Is he okay?"

****

The elevator doors slowly opened, letting Rosie and her parents rush into the ward hall. Their wide, teary eyes fought against the white walls and neon lighting as they hurried to Irma's bedside.

As she approached, Rosie saw that Irma's eyes were swollen and red from crying. Then Irma turned on her side, hiding her face in a pillow. Mother reached for Irma's hand and held it. Dad stood near, gripping the bed rail.

"Irma, Irma, what happened?" Rosie asked. "Tell us what happened."

Irma sobbed into the soft pillow, making sounds that weren't human, so it seemed to Rosie.

"Get her some water." Mother said. "Mi'ja, Irma, we're here for you. Your brother Robert is still at work, but we're all here for you, mi'ja."

Rosie filled a glass with water and handed it to her Mother who put her hand on Irma's shoulder and gently turned her from the pillow. Irma took a small drink, sucked in bits of air, and pounded her cast with a tight fist.

Rosie stood nearby, recalling what her Mother had told her in the car on the way to the hospital: Irma had been visiting Chris all morning because she was worried about him. He just didn't seem to be himself, Irma said, so she sat in her wheelchair next to him, trying to cheer him up. Finally, she asked him if he'd like to see some wheelchair races. Irma was ready to invite the whole ward gang over to get his mind off of things. He seemed so down.

But he said no and that the only company he'd like besides her was his mom. Irma knew his mother lived two hundred miles away and had difficulty getting to the hospital to visit him. Still, she went into action and got the head nurse to help her call Chris's mom and ask if she could come to see her son, Chris, right now, today. Irma handed the phone to the head nurse. She spoke in hush tones and then passed the phone back to Irma. Chris's mother said that she'd be there as soon as possible and thanked Irma for calling.

While they waited, Irma asked Chris if he wanted his nose scratched, but he said no. She stayed with him even when the nurse came in to turn and bathe him inside the iron lung. It was then that she insisted on holding Chris's hand, even though the nurses didn't usually allow it. But the head nurse said it would be okay if Irma wore a surgical glove and only for a minute. So that's what Irma did. After putting the glove on her right hand, she stood up from her wheelchair, reached into the small porthole on the side of the iron lung, and found Chris's hand.

"Cold hand, warm heart, that's what they always say," Irma said to Chris, who gripped the fingers of her hand through the white glove. "Finally, you're smiling."

Soon after, Chris's mother arrived and kissed his forehead. Then, like that, he closed his eyes and didn't wake up. He stopped breathing.

At this moment, with Irma in her Mother's arms, Rosie wanted more than anything to have her sister Irma home.

Chapter Six

Rosie noticed that Miss Glass smiled at her more than usual during class today. Rosie tried to read about the Greek goddess Artemis, but the strong smell of the boys' pomade and drying mucilage glue turned her stomach and made her dizzy. Rosie felt like she had to throw up. She needed air. She needed it now.

"Can I have a hall pass?" Rosie asked as she raised her hand high in the air.

"Do you need to go to the little girls' room?" Miss Glass asked. She reached for a pen.

"Yes, please." Rosie gathered all her strength and walked to the front of the room to get the hall pass, determined not to show how ill she felt. Outside the room, she took in a deep breath now that she was away from classroom odors. She walked down the empty hallway past closed classrooms to the girls' restroom entrance.

Once inside, at the closest sink, Rosie bent over the basin, turned on the water, and splashed her face with cold water. She pulled down a piece of brown paper towel to dry her face. After patting the back of her neck and forehead with the wet towel, Rosie looked into the mirror and noticed her eyes were droopy and her face flush. She waited a few minutes, leaning against the cold tile wall until she felt better. She was about to return to class when the double doors swung open, and in walked Lucha and her gang.

No words were spoken, but the look on Lucha's face reminded Rosie of the time she saw a cat patiently waiting near a mouse hole until the mouse showed itself. Before it could retreat, the cat took a swipe with his paw, sending the dizzy mouse across the floor; then, she pounced on it and ate it.

The girls made their move, circling Rosie, right and left. Rosie held her ground, clenched her fists at her sides, and didn't take her eyes from Lucha. She knew Lucha would make the first move, followed by Cece and the other girls. Lucha would deliver the first blow with her fist, then step back to let the others take their shots. Lucha stepped toward Rosie. Lucha's face was taut and her eyes hard, like polished black stones. She had her right hand in her front jeans pocket; the other dangled at her side.

Rosie stood rigid as Lucha drew close, face to face with Rosie. Rosie brought her right fist up for Lucha to see. Lucha grabbed Rosie's wrist like a vice with her left hand and pulled the fist of her other hand up to Rosie's face.

"Open it," Lucha demanded as she squeezed Rosie's wrist and held it stiff. "Open it."

Rosie tried to pull away but couldn't break Lucha's grip. Rosie felt the blood draining from her clenched fist.

"I said, open it," Lucha ordered with a sly smile that curled her red lips.

Rosie relaxed her fist, and her fingers opened. Then Lucha placed her upturned fist above Rosie's open palm and let small silvery coins fall into it. The metallic jingle sounded like clashing cymbals in Rosie's ears.

"Here's some dimes we want to give you for your sister, Irma, to get better," Lucha said as she curled Rosie's fingers closed and clasped both her hands over Rosie's. "We saved them up, all of us."

Lucha continued to hold Rosie's hand. "It's not much, but…"

"It's a lot." Rosie cut in. "It means a lot."

Lucha turned and walked out the door, followed by her gang.

****

Later that evening at home, Rosie helped Mother cook dinner and set the table, but Manny and Robert were late coming home.

"Why does Grandma Cuca call Dad 'Sevedo'?" Rosie asked her Mother while they stood in the kitchen, waiting.

"Oh, it's nothing." Mother responded. "You know, when we first met, your Dad and me, he was a good dancer."

"For reals?" Rosie asked. "Where did you meet him? Rosie pulled herself up on the kitchen counter to sit.

"Oh, the Avedon Ballroom. He was there with his brothers." Mother began. "I was across the room with my friends, just talking. But we pretended not to see them looking at us, but we knew they were trying to get our attention. Then my friend Letti said that we should be careful because those guys, your Dad, and his brothers, were from a gang called La Loma."

"So, what did you do?" Rosie asked, leaning forward to hear her Mother's soft voice and to watch every look that came across her face.

"Well, what could we do?" Mother asked. "We came to dance. So, when your Dad in his camel coat walked up to me and asked me to dance, I danced."

"When was that?" Rosie asked.

"A long time ago, so long ago, I can hardly remember." Mother responded. "But I do remember one early morning, the day we ran away together, there was an earthquake, un tremblor, that knocked down buildings in L.A."

"You ran away?" Rosie asked. "What did Grandma do?"

"Oh, she was mad. You can't imagine." Mother said. "She sent everybody to look for us until they found us in La Loma, Chavez Ravine, where your Dad's family lived."

"What happened?" Rosie asked.

"Your Grandma," Mother continued. "She came to the house, opened the door, came inside, grabbed me by the hair, and dragged me out and brought me back home."

"What did Daddy do?"

"Manny?" Mother thought a bit. "He sprained his ankle when he jumped out the window, trying to get out of your grandmother's way." Mother laughed and rubbed her teary eyes.

Rosie laughed too as she reached for her Mother and put her arms around her.

"So, maybe that's why she doesn't like him." Mother said. "She always thought he wasn't good enough for me. He has 'old country' ways. He's hard on everybody, hard on himself. That's why she calls him Sevedo."

"Oh." Rosie held on and tried to understand.

"I guess I should have known it would be like this." Mother said. "Lo creo, the earthquake was a sign."

"Mama, do you wish . . ." Rosie began.

"Mi'ja, no. Everything is as it should be." Mother said, taking hold of Rosie. "I love you so much, and Robert, and Irma, and your Daddy. If only . . ."

"If only what, mama?" Rosie pleaded with tears in her eyes.

"If only she, your Grandma, could forgive." Mother whispered. "You know mi'ja, forgiveness is a gift of great value, and it costs nothing."

"Bang!"

"What is that, mama?" Rosie asked, rushing toward the front door. "Someone's outside."

"Rosie, wait." Mother said. "Don't go out there." Mother pulled the curtain back and looked out the window. "It's your Dad's car, but I don't see him."

"Let me see." Rosie ran to the window. "The car lights are still on." Rosie went back to the front door and opened it.

"Don't, mi'ja . . ." Mother was too late. She ran to the door and stood next to Rosie.

Outside they saw Manny sprawled on the ground near the front doorsteps. His face was smiling up at them. He was drunk. He had lost his balance on the first step and fell.

"Manny, where have you been?" Mother asked. "Don't tell me. Tiny's again." Mother turned Rosie. "Help me pick him up."

Rosie and her Mother bent down and gathered Manny's limp body in their arms and led him inside. They sat him in a chair at the table.

"I'll make some coffee." Mother said. "You talk to him."

"Are you all right, Daddy?" Rosie asked. "Do you hurt anywhere?"

"Un cerveza por mi cabeza." Manny sang. "Tu solooo tuuu."

"Manny, be quiet." Mother said. "I'm making your coffee."

"Irma, where's Irma?" Manny asked. "Where's mi'ja?"

"You know where she is." Mother answered from the kitchen. "Don't be crazy."

"Where is she?" Manny asked again, looking past Rosie into the kitchen.

"The County General Hospital." Mother replied, shaking her head.

" Mi hi'ja." Manny began to cry. "Por mi culpa. It's all my fault."

"No, Daddy, it's not your fault." Rosie sat in a chair next to him. "It could have happened to anyone."

"Remember, vieja, I let her go to the plunge all the time before it was closed down." Manny moaned. "She liked to swim and dive off the board, remember."

"Manny, be quiet." Mother said. "It's not your fault. No one knew."

"Mi'ja, Rosie." Manny reached his calloused hand behind Rosie's head and pulled her close. "Promise me that nothing will happen to you. Promise!"

"Oh, Daddy." Rosie threw her arms around him and began to cry. "I promise. I promise."

"Rosie, mi'ja, go to bed." Mother said. "I'll take care of him. You go to bed."

Rosie slowly loosened her arms from around her Dad's neck, went to her Mother, and kissed her on the cheek before she went to her room to sleep.

Chapter Seven

From their room, Rosie and Robert heard Mother's questioning, "Why? Why can't she go?"

"Because I said so, that's why," Dad replied. "Besides, it's not right. It's a boys' show."

"It's a game show for everyone." Mother said. "She should go."

"No, I don't want her to go," Dad said. "And what about Irma, pobrecita?"

"Irma wants Rosie to go." Mother was persistent.

"Maybe, but she's not here." Dad sucked in a breath. "She was supposed to be home tomorrow, remember. But now Doctor Mesmer says no. So, I say no, too. Rosie can't go."

Rosie heard the words and felt their meaning like a blow to her chest. With tears running down her cheeks, she fell into her bed and buried her head in the pillow.

Rosie sat up on the edge of the bed, cradling her head in her hands. Then she closed her eyes and began to see exactly what she had to do---stuff her clothes in a pillowcase, slip out the window like Robert had done so many times before, and follow the footpath to the street. Then run down the alley to the railroad tracks and hop a slow-moving train to anywhere.

"Don't even think about it.' Robert said from the other side of the room. "I can tell you're thinking about running away."

"Stop telling me what I can't do," Rosie said. "Tell me what I can do. I hate him always telling me I can't do this, and I can't do that. I've got to get out of here, away from him. Help me."

"Where do you think you can run to?" Robert asked. "You have nowhere to go. This is your home. There's no place else to go." He ran his fingers through his hair and then rubbed the back of his neck. "Besides, what about mama? You can't hurt her like this. I won't let you. You've got to stick it out, at least till you're older."

"Then what? Get married just to get out of the house, away from him? Is that the only way out?" Rosie asked. She looked at Robert. He looked away.

****

Early next Saturday morning, Robert had already left for work, leaving Rosie alone. Rosie tiptoed to the hole in the curtain and watched her Mother move about the kitchen. Dad sat at the table without breakfast or coffee. Then Mother sat in a chair in the living room and waited for him to speak. He ignored her; she ignored him.

"Go ahead, say what you have to say." Dad looked straight at her.

"Irma says she's praying for Rosie to win the bike." Mother said. "And Grandmother Cuca is coming to pick up Rosie at four o'clock."

"What? Why?" Manny twisted from one side to another in his chair.

"You know why." Mother stood up and walked out of the room.

****

That afternoon, from her room, Rosie heard her Dad's footsteps fall hard and quick in the living room and smelled the smoke from his cigarette. She stood in front of a broken wall mirror, pulling on the sides of her dress as if to stretch them into pants to cover her ankles. Rosie was surprised to see a tall young girl with slender legs in a well-pressed jumper staring back at her. As she brought her ponytails forward over her shoulders,

Rosie stepped closer to make sure she knew who she was looking at.

"Mi'ja, you look bonita. Que linda." Mother said, standing behind her. "Remember, don't change clothes until after they announce your name. I have your overalls in the bag, here."

"What time is it?" Rosie asked. "Are we going to be late?"

"No, no. Your Grandma will be here soon. Don't worry."

"Are you coming with us?" Rosie asked. "You and Daddy?"

"No, but we'll be there later." Mother replied. "Don't worry. We'll be there."

A knock at the door brought a smile to Rosie's face. Her Mother smiled in return, pulled back the curtain, and went to the front door.

Rosie watched as Mother opened the door to greet her mother, Grandma Cuca, with a kiss on the cheek.

"Donde esta?" Grandma Cuca asked. "We don't want to be late." Grandma looked around the room, surprised to find Dad, Severo, asleep, sitting up, on the couch.

"Here, she is." Mother turned to let Grandma Cuca view Rosie, who was coming up from behind her. "Do have everything, mi'ja?"

"Que bonita. Estas lista?" Granma Cuca held Rosie chin in her hand.

Rosie nodded. She was ready to go.

Then Grandma whispered something in Spanish into Quetta's ear.

"Don't worry." Mother said. "We'll be there; we'll both be there."

Rosie reached around her Mother neck and kissed her on the cheek. Then, she ran across the room and kissed Dad on the cheek as he slept with his eyes only half-closed.

Outside, Bertha sat with Don Tosti at the wheel of a new cream-colored Pontiac convertible. Only a city fire engine had more shine to it. In the back seat was Rosie's Abuela, who sat with her head covered in a scarf. Grandma opened the rear door and motioned for Rosie to get in first. Once settled in the comfortable backseat between the two grandmas, Rosie reached forward to shake Don Tosti's hand.

"This is my niece, Rosie," Bertha said to Don Tosti. "I'm her aunt. Can you believe it, for reals?"

"Glad to meet you, Rosie, Rosita." Don Tosti had a deep-toned voice, just like the big bass he played. "A sus ordines." He rolled the Pontiac back on its big balloon tires and then put it in gear with a sudden jolt, sending them off through the courts on the road to Hollywood. Rosie sat quietly beside the two women who held her hands tightly as if they were just launched into the air on the Sky-Ride at the Los Flores Church carnival. Rosie felt the strength in their hands and, looking left and right at their wrinkled faces set to the wind, she thought, "Someday, I want to be like them." At this moment, she felt a part of something bigger than she was--something from long ago, way back before she was born. Maybe it was la familia, that connection, with an unknown beginning and unknown end.

"Listen," Bertha said. "They're playing Tosti's song on the radio." She began to wave her hands in the air and move her body to the beat as the women in the backseat listened and watched.

Chapter Eight

The day had arrived. Rosie sat between Cuca and Abuelita in the backseat of the Oldsmobile. Bertha sat in the front seat next to Tosti, who was driving.

"Are you sure she's competing on the 'Hail the Champ show'?" The studio parking lot attendant looked down from the kiosk at Don Tosti.

"Look, man," Tosti said. "We showed you the studio passes. She's supposed to be in there getting ready right now. So, let us through. We don't want to be late."

"Well, I don't know. The only other ones I let through for this show were boys. She is not going to compete against boys, is she?"

"She'll compete against anybody they put up against her," Tosti said. "Now, let us through, please."

"All right, all right." The gate arm rose, and Tosti drove through to the studio entrance.

Once inside, Grandma Cuca walked to the receptionist, showed the passes, and brought Rosie forward.

"Rosie Diaz. Her name is Rosie Diaz, and she's here to go on the "Hail the Champ" show tonight.

"Well, very good." The blonde lady said. "Rosie, you go through that backstage door on the left. Your family goes to the door on the right and finds a place to sit in the audience."

Grandma Cuca and Abuelita each kissed Rosie's cheeks before they walked away. Then Bertha gave Rosie a tight squeeze as Don Tosti watched.

"Good luck," Bertha said. "And don't worry, your Mother and Dad will be here soon."

"Remember to smile at the camera," Tosti said as he walked away with Bertha, hand in hand.

Rosie waited backstage, thinking about Irma watching at the hospital. She imagined that all the neighborhood kids, including Mundo and Baby Oscar, and their parents were at her house to watch her on television. Her family owned one of only two television sets in Estrada Courts, an eight-inch Tele-King with a chocolate brown plastic cabinet. Dad had to deposit a quarter in a metal box affixed to the back of the set to watch television for an hour. At the end of the week, a collector would come to the house to count the change and credit the amount toward the purchase of the Tele-King.

She knew Robert would be in charge of the grand event. In her mind, she saw him place chairs comfortably around the small screen. Once seated, the neighbors would whisper nervously as the adults drank beer, and the young ones drank Kool-Aid and ate popcorn. After Robert adjusted the rabbit-ear antenna to everyone's satisfaction, they would wait in silence as the snowy picture brightened and the show began.

"Good evening, folks! Welcome to the 'Hail the Champ' show sponsored by the PowerHouse Candy Company." The announcer spoke from the stage to the audience seated in the studio. At the sound of his voice, Rosie snapped out of her reverie. Then the backstage door opened, and Rosie watched her parents as they were escorted in. Rosie's Mother came toward her, hugged, and kissed her for luck. But when she moved toward her Dad, Manny only extended a rigid arm, rested his hand on her shoulder, and said nothing.

"Eight contestants will compete against each other in feats of skill until only one remains the winner." The short, barrel-chested announcer continued in a clear resonant voice. "Now, folks, let's introduce you to our lucky contestants tonight. First, Ralph, age fourteen." Ralph ran onto the stage from the wing and bowed. "Now, Efren, age thirteen, Rosie age twelve, Eddie Twelve, Jimmy, fourteen " Rosie took her bow then ran off stage to change her dress for jeans and a shirt. The announcer introduced the contestants. Then began to explain the rules.

"The contestants will pair up, two by two, to compete in the tire run, the football throw, and the dime bucket-lift. This will be a round-robin. The winners of each pair will compete until there are only two contestants left to vie for the title 'Champ.' All hail, the Champ!"

The stage curtain lifted, revealing Rosie up stage crouched and ready to run. Efren was standing next to her as they both stared down two rows of randomly placed automobile tires, laid out like stepping stones. Rosie and the others faced the task of stepping into the center of each tire as quickly as possible without tripping. The first to reach the finish line at the other end was the winner. All the contestants were lined up with their partners, ready to start.

"Get on your mark, get set, go!" The audience cheered and clapped as the contestants raced across the stage. Rosie lifted her knees high and thought how this was so much like playing hop-scotch at home. She won easily.

"Now, the four winners step over here." The announcer said. "Here they are, folks, the winners of the first round. Let's give them a hand." Rosie noticed a young woman walk across the stage out of view of the TV camera with a sign held above her head that said, "Applause!"

"Now, let's pause for a message from our sponsor, PowerHouse Candy." At that moment, stagehands came out of the wings and set up the next competition—the football toss. They handed Rosie a football and paired her with a tall thirteen-year-old.

"Here we are again, folks." The announcer said after the commercial intermission. "On this round, the boys and girl will try to throw the football across the stage and through the tire hanging by a rope on the other side of the stage. Remember, they have only twenty-five seconds to throw as many footballs as possible through the tire. The person with the most "bulls-eyes" wins. Are you ready? Go!"

Rose gripped the football with her fingertips on the threaded seam like her brother Robert had taught her when she was about nine years old. She cocked her arm so that the ball touched her ear and fired a spiral right through the suspended tire. She made seven out of nine attempts—better than anyone else.

"That's the end of the second round." The announcer said. "Come over here, you two, and what a surprise. Believe me, folks, little Rosie earned the right to be here. She defeated the boys paired with her in feats of athletic skill, the only girl to make it this far. But hold on to your hats; her challenger seems confident. So, let's begin the competition that will decide who will be the next Champ!"

In jeans with zippered pockets and a boy's cotton shirt, Rosie stood next to a table heaped with a mound of shiny dimes, more dimes than she had ever seen in her life. Her opponent, a lanky fourteen-year-old named James, stood next to another table piled with dimes, too.

"Now, listen carefully." The announcer leaned a bit forward to explain the rules. "Here's what you have to do to win in this, the final round called the dime lift. First, you take this scooper and scoop up as many dimes as you can. Then, fill up this empty bucket with as many scoops of dimes as possible. You have only twenty seconds, and the contestant's bucket with the most dimes wins. Easy, right? Just one more thing. You have to lift the full bucket from the table onto the scale, right here." He pressed his fat fingers to the large flat surface of one of the scales to the left of the bucket. The red needle flew around the face of the dial stopping at fifty pounds. "Now remember, the more dimes in the bucket, the more money you get to keep, but the heavier the bucket becomes, the more difficult it is to lift.

And you must be able to lift the dimes to win! Are you ready? Go!"

Rosie took hold of the shiny aluminum scooper that reminded her of Ramos' Market's candy scooper. She dug into the side of the hill of dimes, filling the bowl of the scooper with hundreds of dimes. When Rosie tried to lift the coins into the bucket, she realized she needed both hands to raise the scooper. She got into kind of rhythm, digging into the mound of dimes, lifting the full scooper, and emptying it into the bucket (sometimes spilling coins on the floor), but the clock was ticking. Time was running out.

"Ten, nine, eight," The announcer led the audience in the count down. Rosie emptied her last scoop in the full bucket; then, she grasped the thin wire handle but could not lift it. Had she put too many dimes in it? She glanced over to the other table where James was struggling with his bucket, also. "Seven, six, five . . ."

Rose touched her Santa Maria medal, prayed, and tried again, but nothing. The bucket did not budge. "Fourth, three, . ." Somehow, Rose grabbed the handle with one hand, braced her elbow beneath the handle at a right angle, and then used every muscle in her body to leverage the bucket up and onto the scale.

She looked over to James, who was still unable to lift his bucket. "Two, one…"

"Hail, the Champ!" The announcer grabbed Rosie's arm and raised it into the air. The audience clapped and cheered.

Backstage, Rosie overheard the boy's Dad plead, "How could you let a girl beat you?" But she was feeling proud. She had won the bike. When her parents came to her, Rosie's Mother cried as she swept back invisible strands of hair behind Rosie's ear. At this moment, Manny, brimming with pride, only smiled. For Rosie, that was enough, for now. The sponsor awarded her a bronze trophy, a year's supply of Power House Candy Bars, a Howdy Doody Puppet, a Catalina trip for four, and the Schwinn Roadmaster Bicycle. It was a boy's bike.

"We can give the bike to Robert," Manny said.

"Why can't I keep it?" Rosie argued.

"Because it's a boy's bike."

"I don't care. I can ride it." Rosie's face flushed. She did not want to cry. The tighter she clenched her fists, drew her shoulders rigid, and squeezed her eyes shut, attempting to drive the torrent back, the more quickly the tears made their escape.

"I care. I don't want my daughter riding a boy's bike."

"Can't we have it exchanged for a girl's bike?" Her Mother asked.

"No. I don't know. It's too much trouble. Stop crying."

"Please try, anyway?"

With some reservation, the PowerHouse Candy Company agreed to exchange the boy's bike for a girl's. The company representative made it clear to Rosie that it was not their fault that she, a girl, had won.

Chapter Nine

Weeks before the bike was delivered, Rosie, with Robert and her parents, went to Catalina as guests of the PowerHouse Candy Company. Doctor Mesmer didn't allow Irma to go because she hadn't healed enough yet and had to remain in the hospital.

After walking and sightseeing for hours, they bought some fresh steamed crab legs and sat on the large rocks near the waves.

"I've always wanted to come here." Dad confided, looking around at the harbor.

Rosie sat next to him, feeling so proud. She could tell he was happy.

"I remember all the deliveries headed for Catalina that I'd unload at the docks early afternoons when, on a clear day, you could see it. Oh, the island sitting out there like a castle or something. Boy, I wanted to go there." Dad parted his lips and let his white teeth form a wondrous smile for Rosie.

"It is like a dream," Mother said. "Almost like we've been here before."

"Remember the time I delivered all that Harts Mountain Birdseed to the docks headed for Catalina?" Dad asked in the direction of her Mother. Rosie thought she saw her Mother dip her head in a shy girlish way.

"What happened?" Rosie asked, sensing that her Dad was ready to tell a story.

"Well, this happened before you were born, and Irma was three, and Robert was only one, just a baby. There were many birds for sale at the Harts Mountain warehouse, so I brought one home for your mom. It was a small yellow canary. And a guy there gave me a record of singing canaries that he said would help get her canary to sing."

"Did it sing?" Rosie asked. Mother and Dad only laughed and shared a look into each other's eyes.

"Well, I don't know," Dad continued. "You see, real soon after, the bird in his cage was left out on the porch, and the cat got it. Quick as a wink, it was gone."

"Ohh," Rosie gasped, looking to her Mother for confirmation.

"And your Mother didn't want me to find out, so she played the canary records all the time, especially when I got home from work. Dad laughed. "It was a long time before I figured out what happened."

"I cried when he found out the canary was gone, and I told him everything." Her mom found Manny's hand on hers. "He said, 'It's alright, I'll buy you another one someday.'"

"Did he?" Rosie asked.

"I don't know. All I remember is that he said he would. That was enough."

****

The bike arrived one month later, about the time Irma was finally coming home from the hospital. The V-shaped frame of the girl's model gleamed in mint-green and white strips. Multi-colored streamers dangled from the handgrips above the white side-wall tires that provided a smooth ride. The Roadmaster's accessories included a battery-operated light for night riding and an invisible horn hidden in the frame. The sponsor mounted a wire basket laced with thin, white plastic ribbons to the handlebars because it was a girl's bike.

Rosie was happy. The entire neighborhood gathered around to view the prize that sparkled with its chrome spokes and rims. Rosie's Mother took several photographs of her standing near the Roadmaster before each of the others struck a pose with the bike until the film ran out. Now it was time to test the beauty. Rosie had reserved the first ride for Robert, who mounted the bike by straddling his left leg over the seat.

"I've never ridden a girl's bike before," Robert said. Everyone laughed.

Fifteen minutes later, he returned, welcomed by the applause of twenty kids anxious for their turn.

"It rides real good. Smooth, and it goes pretty fast for a girl's bike," Robert said.

When Rosie mounted the bike for the first time, she did not step into it like a girl. Instead, she straddled her left leg over the seat as her brother had done. In a moment, Rosie took off. She rode the heavy bike stiffly, her back straight and her head high. She rode faster and faster, passing from the dirt paths of Estrada Courts onto the tree-lined streets. Rosie felt the wind sweeping her hair across her face and chilling the beads of sweat there. While her braids wriggled on her back, the air current blasted her cotton shirt tightly against her chest so tightly that she could feel the buttons of the shirt like hard knots against her tender breasts.

Still, she pumped her legs like mechanical cylinders, harder and harder, faster and faster. It was a contest again. Rosie, confident that she could pump and pump until the bike gave out, heard the Roadmaster hum as the tires spun beneath her.

Hazard Hill, that's where I'll take you, Rosie thought. The challenge was on. She headed down the street to the steep incline that even cars shunned.

I know I can do it, said Rosie to herself, standing at the peak and looking down. "Can You?" Rosie addressed her bike as she panted with excitement. "You've got to do it. Robert would have made it if the front wheel of his bike hadn't fallen off. I know we can do it."

Once she nosed the wheel downward, there was no stopping. Brakes were useless. She held tightly to the handle grips and arched her back, seeing nothing but the oil slicks on the blacktop being swallowed by the front tire. Her body relaxed. Feeling like part of the air, now, only a quarter of the way down the hill, she began to pump. The pedals twirled beneath her legs as if detached from the drive chain, and she streaked at a speed that the Schwinn was not meant to travel. She felt she was flying in the arms of some goddess, a protectress. Without fear, Rosie watched the asphalt for sudden holes or cracks that would send her tumbling headlong over the handlebars into the street. No, she mustn't think of that, not now. Nothing can hurt her. She swung her legs forward, removing her feet from the spinning pedals. The bike was coursing freely, and her body, pant-legs flapping, was rushing forward against the wind in perfect faith.

When the bottom came up abruptly, she brought the bike to a gradual halt, dismounted, and screamed.

She had done it. She succeeded where everyone else in the neighborhood had failed. After looking back up the hill, she dashed in front of the bike and held an invisible cape to her side.

"Aye, toro, ay, ay, toro," Rosie enticed like the bullfighter pictured on the calendar at home. She challenged the frozen Roadmaster one more time. "Ay, toro, ay, toro!" she called as she brought the cape high over her head with a smooth pirouette and stood triumphant.

"But girls can't be bullfighters," Rosie said as she slowly stepped into the bike and sat for a while.

Then, riding home, the vision of her Dad, or rather her Dad's arms, was distinct and real in her mind. When she was younger, it had been those sunbaked arms bordered by folded gray sleeves that brought her to his chest where it smelled of tobacco and sweat. There, in the left breast pocket, she would find a stick of Juicy Fruit gum he had saved just for her. Then he would squeeze her, his little girl, tightly.

"Wait till he gets home and sees my new girl's bike." She began to pedal faster. "He'll be proud of me this time. He will."

Later, under a graying sky, Rosie secured her bike to the front door stoop and went inside the house. After eating dinner with Robert and her Mother, she waited in vain for her Dad. Finally, she went to bed.

Once asleep, she dreamed of dancing with a bull in a ring. The crowd watches and cheers as she, wearing silvery ballerina slippers, pirouettes on the sharp tips of the bull's horns. Then she stands on his back as he gallops around the stadium turf. She spins and twirls with ease as his heavy bulk moves along beneath her. Now she stands firmly, reaching with one hand to grasp his tail and, with her other hand, his horns. It's a wonderful trick, and the crowd applauds wildly. Looking down at the bull's head, she notices that between his horns, a wire basket is tied, cradled there with a silver ribbon. Intuitively, she knows that the basket is there to place the flowers that the spectators tossed from the stands. She feels good and happy, wishing she could let everyone know how easy it is to dance with a bull. It's not dangerous at all, she thinks, if you know the secret: "you must never turn your back to the bull."

Now the bull runs faster, and she steps up onto his horns, standing tall, balancing freely with the soles of her feet atop the pointed ivory tips. The excited crowd throws bouquets, filling the ring with color. The bull slows at her command. She leaps to the ground beside him as he stops, and she bows to the people, but as she does, her eyes spy a beautiful bouquet near her. They look like pansies with little children's faces blooming at the center. She must get a closer look. She walks forward to pick them up, forgetting about the secret. Behind her, the bull snorts and stamps. She brings the little faces to her breast and bends her knees to the dirt in a slow curtsy for the young girl in the crowd who threw the flowers down to her. But the young admirer is not smiling. She appears scared. She begins to wave her arms crazily; screaming and yelling fill the air. Then silence. Rosie only hears the churning, rolling charge of the beast at her back. There's nothing to do but wait. She kneels and bows her head into the faces of the children as she feels the silvery wire basket press hard against her back with a loud cracking and crunching of bones.

Her eyes opened. Outside. The noise was coming from outside her window. She looked out and saw her Dad standing there in a light rain in front of his car headlights. He had hit something. Rosie grabbed her bathrobe, putting it on as she ran to the door.

On the front stoop, she met her Dad's eyes that commanded, "Stay inside," but she didn't listen. Looking at the ground in front of the car, she saw her bike beneath the wheels. The bike lay maimed and muddied like a hurt animal. Leaning over the mauled frame, she used her fingernail to clean wet globs of mud from the ribbon-covered wire basket. She knew the damage could not be repaired, but she did not cry.

She felt his hands on her shoulders and heard his voice say, "I'm sorry. I'll buy you another bike someday".

That was enough. Rosie turned and hugged him as she led him to the house and out of the rain. And, besides, Irma was coming home tomorrow, for good.